The Curseborn Saga

NOVELLA III:
THE TWO WORLDS
TOURNAMENT

CREATORS
TROWA D. CLOUD
SQUALL D. ACE
SIMON GATSU SANDOVAL
ELNATH D. SHANKS

WRITER
TROWA D. CLOUD

Created by the Four Lords
Copyright © 2015 by Four Lords, LLC

Excerpt from Novella IV: Falling Tower copyright © 2015 by Four Lords, LLC
All rights reserved.

Published in the United States by The Curseborn Saga, LLC

The Curseborn Saga™ is
a trademark of
the Four Lords, LLC

Four Lords™ is a
trademark of
the Four Lords, LLC

Print ISBN - 978-0-9861939-4-1
eBook ISBN - 978-0-9861939-5-8

Edited by Catherine Knepper
Book Cover Artwork by Jon C. Pool
Book Illustrations by Sean Lam Hayashi
Produced by Elnath D. Shanks
Original Map Design by Trowa D. Cloud
Map Artwork by Sean Lam Hayashi

Official Website | www.curseborn.com
Facebook | www.facebook.com/fourlords
Instagram | @cursebornsaga
Twitter | @cursebornsaga

This book is dedicated to all the great artists of the past,
To all the young artists of the future,
And to all who wish to save the world.

I dedicate this book to the beautiful Kristen Marie.
Your true heart's mirror is fire,
With a soul of wind's beauty.
~ Trowa D. Cloud

To my family, my alpha and my omega.
Without you, there is nothing.
~ Simon Gatsu Sandoval

To my friend Josh Gordon,
Who once saved my life.
I will never forget you.
~ Squall D. Ace

To Nena, no one deserves a love like yours. You give me
strength, you give me purpose. I love you.
~ Elnath D. Shanks

Contents

Novella III:
The Two Worlds Tournament

XXXVI – Brotherhood
– Part IV

… 8 Cycles Ago …

Child Storm ran and ran, dashing through the high blades of grass that surrounded Neverend like a moat of great swaying spearheads. The world was shrouded in a deep shadowy mist. High above, shifting clouds of darkness moved chaotically. Gales churned and rain poured from the sky with a vengeance, as if the heavens above were waging war on Soria. Storm weaved in and out through the trees, running along a path he couldn't see, for the dark of the skies blanketed him under Night's wings.

Present-day Storm sat cross-legged in the sky, gazing down on himself as a child and wondering how it was that he was watching his younger self run through the forest below. *This is my memory*, he finally realized.

Storm watched his younger self run through the towering grey blades and noticed how much shorter he had been—he was just a little runt back then. But why was this memory revealing itself to him now? Suddenly, his eyes widened as he saw the tears in his eyes as a child. He remembered now. That cold night. The harsh rain. The tears. He shuddered as the shadows of his past ran tormented beneath him. And then, as if the memory below were opening its arms to him, Storm felt himself pulled forcefully down and into the mind of his younger self. He was eight cycles old and forced to relive once again that fateful night.

–   –   –   –

Everything I know is a lie, his thoughts screamed. *Maybe Caim isn't even my brother … the old man was never our family. I never had a family. Everything is a lie. Why? Why!?*

A thousand voices shrieked in Storm's head, and with every step upon the cold hard ground his mind grew more tormented and dark. It was at that moment that he wished the Edge would come before him, so he could fling himself from its jagged cliff. He found himself hating Caim, not only for his plain stupidity but for his lack of understanding, and for the lie that their lives had been. Maybe it was true that they were not actually brothers. One of the voices in his head rose above the din, and pointed out that the color of their hair revealed the only truth he could rely on—they were not brothers and the old man had been lying to them all along. Caim was too stupid to see the truth, but Storm wouldn't be tricked. Turning his eyes to the darkness of the treetops Storm released a gut-wrenching scream as loud as his lungs would allow until his voice broke and he crumbled to his knees.

Storm cried out as one might before his own execution, or upon seeing a loved one die before his eyes. He cried and screamed and smashed his fists into the dirt. The knuckles split one by one and the blood of his wounds streamed down his wrists. He could hardly feel any pain at all. He pounded and punched until he could see the white of the bone protruding beneath his torn knuckles. He screamed until his voice faded and ceased, until his hair was matted to his face, and the tears that streamed down his cheeks had formed a glassy black puddle in the mud.

It was then that Storm's eyes found their way to the center of the black puddle of tears. A shimmer of his reflection was whispering at him, attempting to reveal something he could not make out. Gazing closer, the beating of his heart nearly stopped as the puddle became clear: the reflection grinning up at him from ear to ear, with tears of blood, was not him, yet it was. The young boy had hair that fell in the exact same shape and form of his own but was colored like white snow. Its eyes were deep and hollow, and glowed not with a shade of emerald but with a fiery red forged from the cavernous pits of a long-raging inferno. Storm lurched backwards and fell, gasping for air. After many long minutes of trying to calm himself Storm began to breathe easier, and in the quiet, he felt as if something were calling him. He inched his way back to the puddle and summoned the courage to look again.

Now his reflection looked as it always did, with black wet hair falling down his forehead and emerald eyes dim in the dark. Still, his expression was of sorrow and fear and anger, and he felt as if he had aged many cycles in the last few moments. He slapped the puddle, obliterating all images, and lifted his eyes. The trees were far taller than what he was accustomed to, and he had no idea where he was, nor how long or in what direction he had run. A paralyzing pressure seemed to press in around him. Other than the trickle of rain passing through the tree leaves, all was silent. He turned round and round from tree to darkened tree, but the path from whence he'd come was naught to be found. The shadowed trunks of the great trees seemed to grow closer and taller, until suddenly, his gaze fell upon two gleaming crimson eyes that pierced the depths of the blackness.

"W-who's there?!" called Storm. Angry yet mostly terrified, he stared at the two fiery jewels that were growing larger, inching closer. Just as he was about to run, a powerful black leg lined with hardened scales of polished midnight and claws that glowed of silver passed into the moonlight.

The great black beast edged its way past the cover of the trees with unmistakable authority and a presence of pure bloodlust that made Storm freeze. The stare of its fire-lit eyes was deathly, leaving him cold and numb. Storm tried to move backwards but found he could barely keep his balance and the strength in his limbs had all but faded. The beast's claws punctured the ground as it walked and the rain that had fallen on its black scales made them glimmer in the faint light. Its lips were curled back revealing its bladed white fangs, and soon Storm was able to see the fullness of the beast. Its forearms were powerful and thick as tree trunks, with curled black wings reaching out to its sides; its tail was long, serpentine and lined with jagged black spikes all the way to the end. A putrid odor filled the clearing, roiling his stomach with nausea. He could see dark, poisonous ooze dripping from the ends of its tail spikes. Storm remembered the statue of the great beast constructed in the middle of Mako and the little wooden creature Dewey had been playing with in the Colossus Hunters shop. With dawning hopelessness, Storm understood that this creature was the fabled Kushala Flare, the beast responsible for the death of Dewey's father.

Storm started moving backward, ever so slowly and in perfect sync with the beast as it crept toward him. After a dozen steps he found himself cornered, his back against one of the massive tree trunks. And still the trees seemed to inch closer together, as if they were in league with the beast, or were being controlled by it somehow.

Then, for the first time, Storm felt truly alone. After everything—after all the things he'd said and done—he'd ended up here with no friends, and no family. He was fated to die alone.

Where was his family now? *Family*—that's the word Caim and their old man used with such purpose, as if they were a *real* family that lived to protect one another. Thoughts of giving up hung in Storm's mind like a hook. He felt the last of his strength fading, and the fight to continue living grew painfully distant – his secret longing had come before him, and he no longer needed to make it to the Edge to end his pain and misery. After what he had said to Caim, he knew there would be none that would come to save him. He didn't have a mother nor a father to protect him in his time of need. His life had been one of survival and reclusiveness, and now he would die alone. He cursed his cruel fate.

The great beast came forward until it was only a few feet away, then paused as if confused—it had probably never encountered prey that didn't try to run or fight, prey that just waited lifelessly for death. As Storm began to accept his death, his fears dwindled. Then without warning, thoughts of Caim came to his mind – all the times they had played together in the woods, carving swords out of tree branches, only to get into some kind of trouble with their old man for wandering too far or doing something dangerous ... all of the stupid things they had done together, and even though they were beyond silly and infuriating, Caim's antics had always bathed Storm in a light that kept him going, encouraging him to always be strong. In that moment Storm realized that deep beneath his desire to be the greatest swordsman ever, he had always trained hard in order to protect his brother. Bumbling, silly, gullible Caim, who needed a protector if anyone did. And now he had failed Caim. Now who would protect him? His eyes closed involuntarily and in one anguished cry he gave voice to the pain in his soul.

"Caaaim!"

Storm felt a massive force strike his side like a hammer and his consciousness started slipping away. He felt his body slam, hard, into something thick and unforgiving. He keeled over, unable to move. The ground was cold and wet on his face and the ribs in his left side had been cracked and broken. He could feel the footsteps of the beast inching closer and shaking the world around him. His breathing slowed.

"I'm ... sorry Caim," he said faintly, not sure if he was speaking or thinking. And then, all grew dark as his eyes closed for the last time. A vast realm of blackness consumed his mind and his body, and he felt as if he were floating, high in the reaches of thick, heavy space. Pricks of celestial light shone from all places, and he thought he heard a voice calling him, soft and serene in the night, as if the words had been spoken to him many long cycles before, or they existed as some dream that he had never awoken from.

"Storm … Storm, wake up!"

The voice was soft on his ears and sounded like it was echoing across a valley hundreds of leagues away. The pricks of faint light started kindling and their ardent glow illuminated his dark mind.

"Storm!" The voice grew louder and sharper and his senses began to sharpen. The vast blackness seemed to be flowing outwards, like the power of the Sun battling Night for Day's coming.

"Storm! Wake up!"

Storm opened his eyes. Looming above him was a dim silhouette. It was cloaked in beaming light, and the warmth of Day seemed to support it with all its strength. The sky was bright white beyond the silhouette, and as his eyes adjusted he found himself staring into two big blue eyes.

"Caim?" he whispered.

He blinked rapidly and then everything fell dark again. The bright white sky beyond Caim gave way to darkness and towering trees. Again Storm felt rain heavy on his body, and a searing pain from his side. He convulsed and spewed a mouthful of vomit on the ground. Coughing, he looked up. Caim's hair was matted with dirt and rain and blood. The scent of blood was strong upon him and Storm's vision cleared. Caim was quite small in size, still wearing an old tunic of their old man's that hung on him like a dress. Despite knowing he was reliving the memory of that night, he had no control of the events unfolding before him.

"You idiot …" Storm managed a faint whisper.

"Storm! You have to get up! We have to go, that monster is coming!" Storm felt the trunk of a tree behind him and looked around. The trees were not as they seemed before and he realized that he was not where he had fallen and lost consciousness.

"What happened?" he said wearily. He saw that Caim

was holding a long straight silver blade, and the tip of it was coated with black blood, the same blood that was splattered on Caim's face. He recognized the sword as the one from the *Colossus Hunters* shop.

"Storm, we have to go now!" said Caim, who had been glancing frantically into the forest every few seconds.

A sudden bone-chilling roar erupted from somewhere close. It was all he needed to snap back to his senses. The black beast, the Kushala Flare, was nearby, and somehow, Caim had found him and saved him … at least for now. He felt Caim's hand wrap around his side and lift him to his feet.

"Can you run?"

Storm tried to move forward and felt a deep, grinding crack from one of his ribs. He let out a loud cry and tumbled back to the ground. Running his hand cautiously over his side, he found that it was soft and sensitive to the touch and one of the bones was completely out of place. Several of his ribs had been cracked.

"How did you find me?" muttered Storm.

Caim cast a quick glance back to the Forest. "You were screaming … and I heard you."

Storm's eyes grew cold. "Why did you come, Caim? I didn't ask you to save me …" His voice grew to a murmur, "we're not even real brothers –" Storm felt a sudden force strike his face. Hard.

"Sometimes you are so stupid!" yelled Caim, reeling back his fist.

Anger surged through him but knowing he deserved the punch, Storm didn't move or speak. A tear fell down his cheek.

"We have to get back to the town," said Caim, glancing nervously toward the path of escape. Just then, a second thundering roar, this time much closer, shook the trees and the ground and birds took flight in haste. "You'll never be able to run," Caim said. "Here, get on my back."

"Caim, run."

"Storm, there isn't time! I carried you here so don't be stubborn, stupid!"

"I can do it, just give me a–" Storm froze as the same black shadow stalked slowly out of the line of thick trees and came before them. Caim whirled around and raised the sword.

Storm suddenly felt heavy as Caim let go of him. He could barely hold his balance and tumbled backwards. The shallow gasps he could manage didn't afford him nearly enough oxygen. Gazing forward through half closed eyes, he could see where Caim's sword had pierced the beast, right under its breastplate, and black blood was seeping and staining the ground where it walked. There was a look in the creature's eyes that spoke of the deepest hatred, and Storm could feel a chill colder than ice in his bones.

Caim stood still, holding the blade out before him that kept the monster at bay. It circled about him trying to close in on Storm, but Caim wouldn't let it come close. A sinister snarl ripped through its clenched jaw, and its bladed teeth shone brightly as the beast snapped at the air before Caim. Storm tried to calm his breathing and think of a way out of their situation. He looked around at the trees, and at the path Caim kept looking towards, but he knew there was no escape, not in his condition. With his wounds, he would be lucky to get back to the town *without* a Kushala Flare hunting them. He took a deep breath.

"Caim – why did you come for me?"

"Are you kidding? You want to talk right now!?" The beast lunged forward and snapped at the air, but the point of Caim's blade held it back once again.

"But … after everything I said …"

"I don't care what you said Storm, we're brothers no matter what. Don't you get it? Family isn't about blood or having parents or not having parents, it's about caring about the people you care about no matter what and protecting them and loving them and that's that. I don't care if I have silver hair and you have black hair, or we have no parents …" He lunged at the beast again. "We *do* have each other, and you are my family, along with grandpa!" Caim risked a glance at Storm. "And don't even think about giving up, Storm—I'm not giving up, ever! So don't be weak!!!"

Storm felt a surge of tears stream forth from his eyes, and he turned his head away from his brother. He bit his lip desperately attempting to hold them back. But to no avail. The tears were flowing, strong and true. Even after all his stupid antics, Caim understood some things better than anyone else.

Storm detected a sudden movement from the corner of his eye. A burst of hope surged through him—could this be the Hunters of the village coming for them, as they had for Dewey's father? But the light of hope soon faded: out of the depths of the forest stalked a second, much grander and much more terrifying Kushala Flare that showed no fear of Caim or his little silver sword. The horns on its head were long and curved and rolled about as if they were forming a crown of thick, sharp bone. It smashed its tail through three trees as if they were blades of grass. Moving over the fallen trees, its powerful grasp clenched tightly and cracked and splintered the trunks with ease. With a space cleared for its massive body, which was at least twice the size of the first Kushala Flare, it took its place in the center of the clearing and released a thundering roar. Storm noticed a patch of snow white fur glistening on the chest of the beast. He felt that if there was ever a King of the Flares, it had now come before them.

Caim emitted a low moan of despair that frightened Storm more than anything thus far. He watched as Caim faced the enormous black beast that treaded fearlessly until it was towering not only over the smaller Kushala Flare, which now appeared weak in comparison, but over Caim, who had turned to point his blade of silver steel at their new enemy. They were but ants before such a force, so ancestral and full of raging bloodlust that Storm felt as if Soria itself had turned its greatest weapon upon them.

Storm watched fearfully as the great black beast stood beside the smaller Kushala Flare and rubbed its giant snout, jaws lined with teeth – each the size of Caim's blade – across the wound of its kin. Then with a quick butt of its scaled head, it rammed the smaller Flare to the side and snarled menacingly at Caim, who didn't budge, but turned his body so that he stood directly between Storm and the two beasts. And then a dark, growling voice kindled to life out of the darkness of Storm's thoughts. This was an all-new torment—he felt like he was no longer in control of his own mind.

"It has been many winters since the Fangless have come to threaten one of my kind.... I came, hoping for another battle of death and blood, for the cries of my brethren echoed through our land. And so I ran, fastest as I am of the Chosen Creatures, to the aid one of us who is threatened by those unworthy of my presence ... and what do I discover but two newborn Fangless, one wielding a shiny plaything, and one unable to move, or run, or cry for the help of those who will not come. This is our land, and despite your crafted Fangs, this will always be our land. Your blood and bones will be the price you pay for wounding us and it will be a reminder to all Fangless that the lands beyond your world belong only to us."

Caim nearly dropped his sword, and with a sudden movement that caused both of the black beasts to snap their heads towards him, he reached out his free hand and pointed straight at the biggest one.

"DID YOU JUST TALK!?" he cried.

Storm nearly fell over—Caim's idiocy was staggering. Caim spun to face Storm, "That is so cool!!!"

"That is *not* cool!" Storm cried back, clutching his side.

The Flare that had spoken snapped its teeth in the air, and let out a vicious roar that seemed to shake the world.

"You and your ignorant Fangless, reckoning you are the only ones of intelligence in this great world! We have been here since nigh the beginning of time, lurking in the shadows and feasting on your flesh for many winters past. Not only are we of higher intelligence than you, the ones who believe they control this world, but we are named of power ... I am Kreitos, born of Beliosr the Great, who is Master of the Forest."

Caim scratched his head. "Born of the Master of the Forest? You sure you're not just a really big Tree Spirit?" He raised both his arms, "you look like a gigantic Tree Spirit!"

The two beasts moved forward a step and released wrathful snarls.

"Whoa!" Caim cried, placing the sword between them. "You look like one!"

Storm groaned in frustration. "Great, now we are definitely going to die." A strange sense of deliriousness came over him and he almost laughed.

"And why do you keep calling us Fangless?" asked Caim. He pulled up the side of his lip, revealing one sharpened fang. "See, I have fangs too!"

The beasts seemed to grumble at his response, and the sound hummed in accordance with one another. For a second, Storm thought that they were laughing.

"It seems I may have been wrong about your fear of us, Silvers Fangless, for it is the first time one of your kind has compared Fangs with our own. Yet, it is exactly that ignorance that will be your undoing, for now I must accept your challenge and you will draw your Fangs against my own. I will not find rest until I have chewed your bones to dust and drunk my fill of your blood."

With that Kreitos lunged forward with such speed that Caim had no time to respond. With a swift swipe of his massive paw, the Flare sent Caim's body catapulting sideways into a tree. The sound of Caim's body cracking was horrible in Storm's ears. Caim struck the tree nearly ten feet up and slid slowly down its side until he collapsed at the bottom. His head slumped down and his eyes closed.

"CAIM!" screamed Storm in terror.

Storm stared at the two beasts that came to stand in the center where Caim had been, their gaze flickering back and forth between the two brothers. They turned their heads in Storm's direction, as if they had found the scent of his blood overpowering and it was drawing them closer. They stalked toward him and his breath grew heavy and quick and his palms began to sweat; the hairs on the back of his neck pricked upwards sharply. He tried to move but couldn't, and neither could he break his gaze with the flaring crimson eyes of the beasts. They were within feet of him and the smaller one had come forward, as if he was bent on avenging himself with the first kill. The smell of its breath was putrid and smarted Storm's senses and just as the beast opened its sword-lined jaw, he heard a sudden pain-filled cry.

The two beasts turned around and there between their huge hulking bodies of black rippling scales, Storm could see Caim. Storm's eyes grew wide and he cried out in sudden fear and despair: he was about to watch his brother die before his eyes. Caim was sitting by the tree with a grin on his face, yet blood was flowing openly from his side, for the sword he had held in his hand had now been thrust into his stomach—by his own hand.

"You bastards like the blood, don't you!" screamed Caim. He coughed and blood sputtered from his lips. "Come on then! I'm right here!" His head bobbed up and down as if he were passing in and out of consciousness.

"Caim, are you crazy!?" screamed Storm. "What the hell are you thinking!?" Even as he was speaking, the two beasts were twisting around to face Caim, the smell of his blood provoking their visceral instincts to rip him limb from limb.

"Storm—run!" screamed Caim, but his voice faded at the end and he grew silent. Storm stared into the eyes of his brother. He slowly took in the whole sight, running his eyes over the sword wound. Storm didn't know what to do, what to think. And then he saw it.

Run, was the word Caim mouthed before his eyes closed.

Only his smile remained.

Storm struck the ground with his fists and screamed desperately in an attempt to draw the attention of the Kushala Flare, but to no avail. They were nearly upon Caim and he knew they would not listen to his cries. Anger flowed through his veins. Everything was his fault. He had run into the forest because he had allowed his own emotions to overcome him. Caim had saved his life already once today, despite all the horrible things he had said to him. As his anger swelled, something grew fiercely from deep within his body, and a refulgent aura of crimson flame burst forth from him, singeing and setting aflame the tree trunk at his back. The pain in his body, the broken ribs, his shattered knuckles and even his broken mind—nothing mattered. The fiercer the aura grew, the more strength returned to him ... and then, as if a long suppressed lock upon his mind was cracked, he pulled the aura back into his body by instinct alone, and felt the pure power flood his bloodstream. The pain was overwhelming, far worse than the pain of his broken bones. It was as if he were being torn apart from the inside out, and the sound of his screams, horrible and deathly in the darkness, caused the two beasts to stop and turn.

But they saw nothing except a faint trace of silvery mist.

Storm moved like a blur across the clearing, darting between the legs of the massive creatures. He spanned the entire gap between him and Caim in the half second it took for the two beasts to begin to turn their heads. By the time they were looking at the place he once sat, he was holding Caim in his arms. An aura like crimson fire was engulfing Storm's entire body, and wisps of hot steam were leaking from his arms.

"You idiot," he said, but Caim didn't answer. He wrenched the sword from his brother's stomach and tossed it to the ground. Lifting Caim, he could suddenly feel the anger of the beasts clearly as if he had become attuned with their emotions, and without looking, knew they had just sensed what had happened. With his newfound speed and power, Storm grasped his brother and Flashed through the thicket of trees. Seconds later, he could hear the roars of the beasts and the shaking of the ground from their crashing pursuit.

"You will not escape us, Silvers Fangless, Black Rains!"

Storm looked down at Caim, whose blood had soaked his hands and arms. "Don't die on me, brother!"

Storm flashed through the trees with such speed that the two beasts could not gain on him. His unlocked ability gave him incredible strength and agility, and it felt like fire had replaced his blood. He turned his gaze in the direction Caim had once looked – the direction of Mako hopefully – and continued Flashing like a crimson blur through the underbrush. He would run to the end of the world if he had to – he would save his brother no matter what.

Then, as suddenly as the unlocking of his Limit Seal had happened, it vanished. The steam faded along with the flames.

Immediately, Storm tripped and stumbled to the ground, crashing hard. He held on to Caim with all that was left of his strength and the pain of his broken ribs seemed to grow a hundredfold, as if they were being broken a second time. Fatigue surged through him and he fought with all his might for his consciousness, for he knew if he lost that, all would be over. Blood started leaking from his pores where he wasn't previously injured.

Storm's breathing quickly grew heavy and staggered and he held his brother in his arms as he felt the quaking of the ground grow more forceful, until the two black beasts emerged out of the clearing of trees. He grabbed Caim and stared up into the daunting red eyes once again. They were running towards him, teeth flared, determined not to let anything get in their way again. Storm looked at his brother one last time, and hated himself for being so selfish and foolish. He wanted to apologize, to live with his brother and see him smile again, but the thought seemed distant and fading and he at last came to terms with his fate.

"At least we die together," whispered Storm. The cold wind rustled past his face as if it were soothing him. He could nearly feel the hot breath of the Flares upon him.

"Since when did I teach you to ever give up?"

The voice was commanding and full of power. Storm knew the voice, for he had heard it his entire life. At that moment the two beasts came to a sliding halt and he felt someone walk by him. A black flowing cloak billowed out from behind the old man as he stepped between the two brothers and the two beasts, which eyed him cautiously. Then the voice of the Flare came again, like a shadow in the corner of a white-lit room until all was consumed by it.

"*Leave us be, old foe! These newborn Fangless have insulted our kind and injured my brethren. They will pay with their blood and bones. Leave us, you wandering Ghost of the Forest. You make a habit of appearing in places where you are not to be concerned. This is our land!*"

"*Ghost of the Forest?*" asked Ronin. "I don't know … but I like the sound of that." He drew his cane from his cloak and from it, a long sleek blade that glowed blue in the light. The two beasts didn't move but eyed his blade warily. Storm, on the verge of collapse and struggling to maintain consciousness, could not understand why they were not attacking him.

"I am sure I appear in many places where I am not to be concerned," said Ronin, "but in this place and in this moment, this is my only concern. This is my family you hunt, my two boys, and although they are young in mind and reckless, I will not let you taste even a drop of their blood." A sudden powerful force emanated from Ronin's body and swept over Storm with a warm feeling, although it had the opposite effect on the Kushala Flares. They roared loudly but did not move so much as an inch toward Ronin, as if some impenetrable barrier were obstructing them.

"You cannot defeat me ... that you know," said Ronin. "Now be gone! I do not wish to draw blood with the Master of the Forest's kin." Ronin bowed his head to the creatures whose glares were full of contempt and frustration.

"*We will not forget this, Old One ... of what you are, we do not know, but since your coming into our land many winters ago, you have respected our kind and we have not crossed paths of blood. But to call these Fangless your kin is a lie that we see without hindrance ... we will be watching you.*"

"And I you," said Ronin. "For these boys are my family, whether you can understand that or not." At the sound of these words, a blanket of warmth and hope enveloped Storm's mind, and his consciousness was finally taken from him.

XXXVII – Brotherhood – Part V

… 8 Cycles Ago …

Storm felt as if he were falling in and out of consciousness for a time undeterminable. All he knew was that a strong arm was wrapped around his torso and he was hanging at the mercy of that arm, with his eyes pointed to the ground, for he wearily opened them here and there only to see traces of grass and stone and darkened roots. The energy of his body had been completely depleted and the pain of his wounds steadily worsened as they traveled, as if with each step his ribs cracked a bit further. His head grew hot and sweaty and a fever swept over him. He dreamed of cold water to rest in. With a sudden jerk, he found himself tossed through the air as if in slow motion, flying through the skies head over heels until a *blast* of freezing cold water came over him. He opened his eyes ready to fight anyone and anything until he realized he was completely underwater. Choking back his wasted breaths, he turned to the faint silver light above and swam upwards to the surface, exploding out of the water like a flying fish.

"WHAT THE HECK —" he screamed, rising out of the water. He saw his old man sitting on the ground next to a great warm fire in the dead of night. Ronin was staring upwards at the many stars pricking the dark skies. "Are you crazy!?" screamed Storm, falling back in the water.

Beside him he saw an uprising of bubbles and braced himself, only to find Caim shoot out of the icy cold water a second later.

"Whoever threw me in here is dead!" screamed Caim, who had swum up so fast that his entire body had burst forth from the lake. Caim stared evilly at Storm, immediately suspecting him.

"I'm in the water too, you moron," said Storm.

"If I hadn't thrown you in the water, you really would be dead," said Ronin with a grave voice.

Storm looked around and found that they were floating in the great lake; it gleamed of crystal in the starlight. He stared in wonder until his eyes fell upon the great towering tree that seemed to rise out of the lake as if it were still growing. It glittered in the distance like thousands of ardent stars in the night, and Storm did not know how such a tree could glow brighter than the stars. Neverend was dark and towering in the distance and the breeze that rolled past him was warm and soothing. Moving his hand to his side, he felt that his ribs were healing before his eyes and that faint traces of emerald green energy were rising all around him and Caim, casting spirited reflections on the water. His fatigue and fever had nearly vanished and he felt like he had just slept for many days and nights. He was completely revived. He quickly looked towards Caim seeking his sword wound, but it had completely disappeared as well, and Caim was already crawling out of the water.

"Thanks for saving us grandpa, I knew you would!" Caim shook out his hair like an animal.

"Like you did," said Storm, quietly.

"Of course I did, stupid!" said Caim, turning around and sticking his tongue out.

"Then why did you stab yourself!?" yelled Storm.

Caim's eyes widened. "I stabbed myself!? Ahhhh!!! I should be dead!" His little hands ran across his body. "STORM!" He turned suddenly. "I must have a new power!" His face became serious, "I definitely have a new—"

CRACK!

Storm uppercut Caim straight in the chin, watching in glee as he spun upwards in the air and landed back in the lake.

SPLASH!

Storm turned to face Ronin, but the old man's eyes were stolen by the stars and his ears were not heeding their words. The lines in his face were dark and prominent, and Storm felt that he was much older than he looked. His cane was resting on the ground beside him and both of his hands were clenched together.

"YOU'LL PAY FOR THAT!" screamed Caim as he launched out of the lake. But Storm didn't move. He didn't know what to say or do, watching the old man before him in silence. Caim came to a stop, watching Ronin who was completely silent.

Raising his arms and yawning, Caim walked closer. "I'm tired," he said. He settled next to the fire, and soon fell asleep. Storm sat still for a very long time accepting the silence before he heard Ronin speak.

"I have something for you boys."

Storm opened his eyes and realized that he had drifted into a light sleep for many shades, for the moons were no longer shining above like crystals and the orange glow of the rising sun was coming upon the distant horizon, throwing powerful spears of fire towards the looming darkness.

Caim opened his eyes sleepily and rubbed them, trying to rouse himself. "Is it food?"

"No Caim ... but it is something I should have given you many cycles ago, when you were younger, for they are not mine to keep but yours ... they are the only gifts your parents left you."

"From our parents?" asked Caim, sitting up. Storm held

his breath, wondering what it could be.

Ronin nodded. "But, before I give them to you …" He looked at Storm, who didn't shy away from his eyes no matter how much he wanted to. "I want to say I'm sorry … what happened earlier was my fault. You are my family, though not by blood … and my hesitation towards telling you boys the truth led to much pain and suffering for you … and I hope, that one day, you can forgive me." He looked deeply at Storm.

"What happened to the black beasts?" asked Caim.

"They have returned to Neverend," said Ronin, not yet looking away from Storm. "But be wary of them, for they are prideful and will not forget this night for many winters, if ever." Storm's eyes lifted at the old man's use of the word *winters*. In some ways, he spoke like the Flares.

With that Ronin pulled something out of his pockets and held his hand out before him. Storm peered closer and saw two shimmering silver chains that glowed like molten fire under the distant sunrise.

"Even though your parents do not live with you today … they did leave you with something that you will always have. Your names." He offered one of the silver chains to Caim and placed the other in Storm's palm. It was oddly heavy and felt to Storm as if the silver chains contained a weight not seen by their appearance. Storm ran his fingers over the bracelet and found that there was something etched into one of the links. They were runes that he could make out and with them, he slowly spelled his name and clenched his teeth, but even with all his might, he could not stop the tears that fell down his cheeks.

They sat together in silence until the rising Sun had fully shown her face on the horizon. Storm reached to the clasp of the necklace and hung it around his neck. He took a deep breath. "Then we are … brothers, by blood?" It seemed as if a great weight had been lifted off of him.

Ronin's face was like stone. "Even if it's not proven by these chains of the past, you are brothers. To be truly brothers is something that goes beyond blood, it's an unbreakable bond forged through years of pain, love and acceptance."

nd although Storm did not respond, he felt like all the warmth of the sun could not overtake the feeling in his heart. Regret and sadness swept over him for what he had said to Caim out of anger. For many moments he pondered quietly, and then a question truer to his soul than any other awoke in his heart.

"Do you think they are still alive?"

Ronin took a breath. "I'm sorry, Storm, for I know nothing. All I was left with were these bracelets engraved with your names. Yet, there are clues hidden within these chains. If they were crafted by your parents, then that would mean they were either Jewelers or perhaps Blacksmiths." He paused. "There is also the mystery behind your names."

"Our names?" asked Storm.

"Caim and Storm were once heroes of the past … legends who fought against the God of Death in the early times of Soria. Firstborn brothers, they were inseparable."

"Cool!" said Caim, his eyes gleaming. "One day we'll be heroes too!"

"What does that mean though? I mean, why is that mysterious?" asked Storm.

"It means that most likely your father was one who lived by the sword. But it also means he was likely a rebel. Those of Falia have stopped naming their children after heroes long ago, for fear that their hopes can never come true. It is widely believed that only those of Risia can be born heroes, unfortunately."

Storm took a deep breath. "Why would anyone think that?"

"I bet our dad was the strongest swordsman ever!" interrupted Caim. Storm smiled slightly at the thought of their father being someone of importance and strength.

Ronin grew quiet and seemed to be pondering something deep within his mind. Storm sat for a while, also deep in thought, wondering if his parents had indeed been Jewelers or

Blacksmiths or even Swordsmen, and often found his fingers touching the silver chain hanging from his neck. He felt as if a sudden piece of his heart had been filled, and with the silver chain, a sense of truth that he had long sought was now found. Yet, he wouldn't give up and he would search for more truth about his parents and why they had abandoned them. He suddenly felt a hand on his shoulder and looked up to see Caim looking down at him.

"Let's look for our parents together!" His smile was pure and bright and curved from ear to ear. Storm nodded without speaking, biting his lip and trying not to cry. Caim reached into his pocket and Storm froze, for out he pulled a sugared brown cookie shaped of the moon and handed it to him. Storm suddenly felt very foolish but smiled faintly at Caim as he took and bit into the wet and crumbling cookie. The taste would have been unforgettable even if it were made of dirt.

"Thanks ..." whispered Storm. He looked Caim in the eye. "Brother."

Caim smiled openly and nodded his head.

"I shall also help you, however I can," Ronin interceded, standing up. "I will help you uncover the mysteries of your past. But for now, sleep. It is has been a long night." With that, Storm lay on his back and rested his eyes, and before he knew it he had fallen into a deep slumber. That night he dreamt of the parents he never knew.

XXXVIII – A Pouch of Golden Coins

DING!

Storm's eyes shot open. His whole body was sweating and his heart racing. He wanted to punch something, anything. He sat up quickly, his eyes glaring violently at the bell that had awoken him from his slumber.

DING!

The sound of the golden bell reverberated throughout their tiny chambers. Storm's hands quickly covered his ears, and he tried with all his might to drown out the crushing sound.

"I told you this was a bad idea!" shouted Storm, but his voice was drowned out by another loud *DING*. He decided to just close his eyes and covered his ears until it stopped. After what seemed like half a minute the ringing had stopped, although he was still wary to uncover his ears.

With a deep breath and a look of frustration, Storm stood to his feet and stretched his arms and legs. It took a while to calm down after awakening from such a dream. His heartbeat wouldn't slow down for many minutes and his anger wasn't quick to cool. He felt strange, and wondered why it was that all these past memories were suddenly flooding back to him, with such vivacity at that. He wondered if there was something within them, something he might not have learned when he first lived them, or something he might have missed, but he could not put his finger on it. The only thing the dream had left him with was a strong feeling of frustration, and no matter how hard he tried, or how ridiculous he knew it was, he realized his frustration was directed at Caim.

"Speaking of which…" he muttered. Storm walked around the golden bell, stopped suddenly, and slapped his hand to his forehead. There, with his arms and legs spread out as if one was sleeping on a bed of fresh grass, was a softly snoring Caim. The great ringing of the bell seemed to have affected him greatly.

"Are you kidding me!?" cried Storm. He knelt down next to Caim and rapped his knuckles against his brother's forehead. "What the hell are you made out of? How could you sleep through that? You literally sleep like you're dead …"

Caim slightly stirred and suddenly jumped. Before Storm could move, he felt a fist connect to his face. He toppled backwards.

"*Get away … dragon … give me back … breakfast*" muttered Caim, bringing his fist back down to his side.

"You little bastard …" said Storm as he rubbed his face. Just when he decided he would go on without Caim and leave his stupid brother in the tower to sleep the day away, Caim sat straight up. He rubbed his eyes and gazed sleepily at Storm.

He spoke with one eye half open, "where'd … the dragon go?"

"You're an idiot," said Storm. "It stole your breakfast and left the tower."

"What!?" cried Caim, jumping to his feet. He immediately felt very dizzy and fell down like a piece of paper. Caim stared up at the stony ceiling while he gathered his thoughts. After a second he raised his fist high into the air. "Wait a second … we don't have any breakfast! We should get some." He stood up attentively.

"You can get breakfast if you want to," said Storm. "I'm going to go win the Soldier Games."

"The Soldier Games!" yelled Caim, sticking his arms in the air. He took a deep breath, "cannot be won without breakfast!!!" He eyed Storm for a moment, watching as his brother neared his leather pouch of silver armor. "You promised," said Caim.

Storm didn't stop moving. "Huh?"

Caim walked to his side and stuck out his fist. "Jonken."

"Why?"

"Jonken."

"Why are we doing Jonken?"

"To see who has to wear the smelly armor."

"They both smell like shit."

"Jonken!" Caim said louder, holding out his hand.

Storm gave in and held out his hand. "Sword beats Dragon. Dragon beats Shield. Shield beats Sword. Don't get mad when you lose."

Caim grinned, "Don't pretend like you're not the sore loser brother."

"Jonken-Po!!!" they shouted in unison, and both made the symbols for Shield with their hands.

"Tie goes once more!" they spoke again and both made the symbol for Dragon.

"Tie goes once more!" they spoke again, and both of them made the symbol for Dragon once again. Storm's eyes grew dark as he watched Caim preparing.

"Tie goes once more!" they yelled. Caim threw the symbol for Dragon, while Storm made the symbol for Sword and it was all over.

"I won …" said Storm solemnly.

"Awww man," said Caim, "I don't wanna wear the stinky armor."

Storm sighed. "Sometimes I wonder why I am so honest … Caim, you never remember anything. You don't have to wear the bad armor, I do."

Caim looked up. "What do you mean, I won?"

"Whoa, don't get ahead of yourself soldier. It's clear you are the loser here. Of the gods, do you really not remember anything that is ever said, like ever? Focus now, stay with me. In losing is winning, or so the old man taught us a long time ago. The winner of the match always performs the losing task. It's because the winner can't gain two wins. By winning the game you have already triumphed once, and claiming the prize on top of that would be too greedy. It is uncharacteristic of swordsmen. With these rules humility is learned and hubris is lost. Therefore, the winner is allowed to be humble in accepting the terms of defeat. A win and a loss for both. It is fair."

"I like this game," said Caim happily, looking at his hands as if he'd had some magic power within them.

"You only like this game when you're the winner," muttered Storm.

"You mean the loser."

"Nope. Not happening. We are not going there." Storm's expression became sour, and he did not speak as Caim grabbed his leather satchel of armor and retreated back to his own corner. A second later, the other bundled pack of armor flew across the chamber and *clinked* to the stone ground before Storm.

"Sometimes I really hate you," said Storm as the armor fell out of the bag. He could smell it from where he stood. Looking down at the stone floor, he saw a small metal can with dried white paint streaking down the sides.

"Hey Caim," Storm said, kneeling down and picking up the cup. "I was able to come across some white paint last night, and I think we should use it to paint our Hollow. Other than the mark on our wrists, it would be the first thing to give us away. Last night, I noticed on the nobles that their hollow was the same color as ivory." He tossed the can to Caim.

It didn't take them long to fasten the armor over their own clothing. The painting of their Hollow had taken slightly longer, and Caim's didn't come out nearly as well as Storm might have hoped, but it'd suffice. They had decided to take the armor from the tallest of the nobles and the fattest, since Anima's armor was much too big for either of them. Caim had been lucky in winning Jonken, and had won the armor of the taller noble. The taller noble seemed to have good hygiene, yet still parts of the armor looked awfully strange on Caim's body; who was able to wear only the helmet, breastplate, pauldrons, bracers and upper greaves. Caim decided against the heavy silver boots and stuck to his wooden sandals, much to the dismay of Storm.

On the other hand, Storm wasn't so fortunate. He was forced to wear the armor from the fattest of the nobles. The armor was thick, heavy and smelled of horrid body odor, a stench that nauseated Storm. The breastplate was enormous and wide, making Storm look huge himself; the greaves were too short for his legs and made him look as if the entire proportions of his body had been off since birth, while the black of his own clothing peeked out in numerous places. He felt slightly better as he pulled his hood out from under the back armor and laid it over his shoulders.

Just breathe slowly … and don't hurt anyone, thought Storm. *The first one to give me crap for this is going down.*

Caim stared transfixed at Storm as he waddled before him; his arms were stuck out to his sides and he could hardly move under the cumbersome armor. Before he could stop himself, Caim was rolling to and fro on the floor laughing hysterically at Storm, who kept tightening his white knuckles.

"Maybe I'll just kill you here and take the armor," muttered Storm. Caim's laughing died down slowly as he stood up, walked over to Storm and slapped him on the shoulder. "There's nothing to be mad about," he said. "It's just … you've become the chubby Boy of Darkness!" He burst out laughing again. Storm reeled his arm back to swing, but the armor impeded him and he ended up rolling into the wall.

Slightly embarrassed, Storm stood and removed his breastplate. He placed it on the ground in front of him. "I've had enough of this," he said. Unsheathing his sword, he slashed twice. Obese chunks of steel clanked to the stone ground. He reattached the breastplate to his chest and fastened it with leather straps.

"Much better," he said.

"You don't look much different," Caim laughed.

"Feels better," answered Storm. "Let's go."

"Wait, wait!" said Caim. "I forgot something. Where did you go last night?"

Storm's eyes were evil and glinting. "Not that you would understand, but I was …" His mind returned to the dark of the forest from the night before. "Skipping stones."

"Skipping stones?" asked Caim. "Bah, whatever. Let's go already!" He lifted the silver winged key and placed it around his neck. Across the chamber Storm did the same.

The sun was wan on the distant horizon and the clouds far away were dark and heavy, moving like a black blur along the edge of their world. The air was chilly and completely different than the day before. A strange icy feeling had come to envelop Trestles. The two brothers were swift and moved silently (at least Caim did) as they left the tower, careful not to let anyone see them leaving. Down below, the walkways were lined with hundreds upon hundreds of Sorians moving and bustling along towards District Four. Then, just as Storm was about to tell Caim his plan for how to get down, Caim stepped forth from the tower and dropped, plummeting like iron falling from the sky. He landed with a heavy *thud* onto the stone below. A little girl looked up in awe as her mother screamed and then fainted. The impact cracked the ground in several directions and sent running a dozen Sorians. Several others looked up at the sky in awe. A second later, Storm landed next to him, creating a much wider and bigger *crack* in the ground as Caim laughed.

"There goes our sneaky entrance," muttered Storm.

As they made their way through the District towards the Fourth, they soon realized that all the Falians around them did not engage in eye contact with them, nor did they *ever* move in front of them or hinder their path. Anger surged in Storm—were the Falians so weak and cowardly that someone merely wearing silver armor would spook them into shameless hiding? Caim waved and smiled at Falians who stared at him strangely.

It wasn't long until the two brothers entered District Four. Across the white courtyard were the great Black Gates, engraved with the symbol of the Empress that seemed to glow red with the rising sun. Storm noticed that the tent had been completely removed and there were no longer any traces of it, as if it had never existed. As they walked across the courtyard, he noticed dozens of Falians wearing hooded cloaks and sitting along the outer walls of the District. They looked like the remnants of a plague that had swept through a town, leaving nothing but silence and sadness. Just before they got to the gate, Storm reached out and stopped Caim.

"Give me the pouch of sori we found last night."

Caim smirked at him, "Ohhh … now you wanna carry it?"

"Just give it to me," Storm said again.

Caim reached to his side and unstrung the clinking pouch of golden coins. He watched Storm waddle away with the money and laughed to himself. Storm came to a stop before a hooded old man sitting on the edge of the courtyard and handed the frail little man the entire pouch of sori. The old man's eyes grew wide with wonder, and he bowed deeply. Caim watched Storm whisper something to the old man, and then watched his brother return.

"What was that?" asked Caim.

"Just a little precaution. Let's go."

As the brothers approached the daunting black gates, a sudden feeling of nervousness swept through Storm. However, Caim felt thrilled, and was exhilarated to see the grand Arena of Kings up close.

"Don't say a word," said Storm. "I'll do the talking."

"Why?"

"Because you're an idiot, and they'll know that."

"You're an idiot," answered Caim, "everyone knows that."

"Seriously Caim, I'm not in the mood." They came to a

stop at the base of the enormous black gates, and, nearly fifty meters above them, from within the two towers that flanked the gate sprang forth two guards. One was beastly with a thick beard, while the other was thin and short.

"Hail, Nobles of Risia!" shouted the bearded man in a child-like voice that made Caim laugh. The two guards at the top of the gate stared down and gave the Sorian salute, to which Caim responded, trying to mimic them, yet failing horribly. The beastly guard raised an eyebrow and Storm's eyes shot sharply to his brother.

"We're here to compete in the Soldier Games!" called Storm.

For a moment, the two guards at the top didn't speak, suspiciously eying the strange-looking nobles.

"The contestants for the Soldier Games should already be gathered at the base of the coliseum," the big guard answered. "What are you two still doing on Falia?"

A few Falians in the courtyard had stopped and were idly watching. This furthered Storm's tension and he knew they had to figure something out fast. He didn't realize that being on Falia might have been something strange for the nobles.

"We were hungry!" shouted Caim, and Storm nearly toppled over.

"I told you to shut up and not say anything," Storm whispered harshly.

The guards were quiet before casting strange glances to one another. Then suddenly, they broke out in laughter and started stamping their spears on the top of the gate. "Last-minute meals before you risk your lives, huh!? I like it!" The beastly guard laughed deeply. "I hate to admit it but those curseborn do make some mean grub!"

Storm's fingers tensed at the words but he didn't move. He resisted every urge to run up to the gates and ... "So, you'll let us pass?" he shouted, a hint of anger in his voice.

The guards stopped laughing and peered at the two of them. "I think we might have to come down and take a look at you two ... you seem a bit...off." Storm sighed as the two nobles moved towards the center platform that would bring them down and all their chances would be over.

"Give me back my sori, you filthy nobles!" A sudden shout echoed across the courtyard and the two guards stopped and looked at the frail robed man who hobbled over and was poking Storm with his cane.

"These two bastards stole from me!" he shouted to the guards on top of the bridge. "Come down here and do something about it!"

Storm completely ignored the irritating pokes of the man's cane. A flicker of a grin curled on the edge of his lip. He waited. Up above, the two guards had frozen stiff and were contemplating the situation. If they went down they would be forced to relieve the two nobles of the sori they had taken, and after looking around, they realized that quite a crowd of curseborn had gathered in the courtyard and were watching. They stopped at the platform and called down.

"Show us the keys and you may pass!"

Storm smiled. His plan had worked perfectly. Reaching to his chest he held up the shimmering silver key shaped like a wing.

"And the other!?" they shouted.

Storm turned to his right. Caim was poking the frail little man in the middle of his forehead. "What are you talking about? I didn't steal anything from you! Liar!"

"Caim, you idiot!" whispered Storm. "Show them your key!"

Caim turned around. "What is this guy talking about, Storm?" His eyes grew wide and then narrowed. "Did you steal his sori!? You evil bastard, Storm. Stealing an old man's sori, you should know better!"

"The other needs to show his key or we're coming down there!" shouted the guards again.

"Caim, don't be stupid! Show them your key and I'll tell you later!"

Caim stared suspiciously at Storm before looking back at the old man who was winking at him.

XXXVIII – A POUCH OF GOLDEN COINS

"I don't get it," said Caim, "but if you did, we're gonna fight." He reached under his breastplate and pulled the winged key out and into the light.

"Very well!" the two guards said, returning to their posts. "You may pass!" As they entered their towers, they placed their hands down on two identical levers and pulled at the same time. All across the courtyard, Falians stopped in awe as the two great black gates boomed and opened. The sound roared like giants walking through their town, their footsteps cracking and breaking the stone as they walked. An icy wind rushed forth through the opening and past Storm and Caim, causing them both to shield their eyes. After the wind passed, the two brothers stared at the ancient stone road that carved its path through the sky.

"This is … the coolest thing ever," whispered Caim.

"I think … you might actually be right for once," answered Storm. It felt as if they were about to embark on a path to a far away, mystical land, as if they were leaving reality and entering a fairy tale.

"This is it," said Caim.

"Yeah," answered Storm, "there's no going back now." There were only two ways this path would lead them, and he didn't want to think about what would happen if they were caught.

"Grandpa is gonna kill us," said Caim, smirking.

"He's gonna have to get in line," grinned Storm.

"You may pass!" shouted the guards, who both came forth to the center of the thin stone carving that connected the two towers at the top of the gates. They watched as Caim and Storm passed through the gates and began walking. Just as they were out of sight, one of the guards squinted down at them. "I think one of them is wearing sandals… ."

"What? No, that can't be," said the other guard. "Nonetheless, I might not be surprised. They were a strange pair, the strangest I've ever seen pass through here in recent. Those were soldiers fighting in the games. I can't believe they asked us if we would let them pass. Was it just me, or did they seem weird to you as well?"

The beastly guard turned and started back to his tower before laughing. "Honestly, you think too hard about things. Perhaps it's the late night drinks and the imaginary boy with silver hair that's distracting your thought process." He smirked. "You know what I think? I think those were a couple of guys who know how to eat!"

XXXIX – The Promise

A day had passed since the three sisters had unexpectedly been called to the Valyti. And it was in the Valyti that they had witnessed things that very few Sorians would ever have the chance to see—the battling for the Rank of Vice Captain between two astonishingly strong powers: Lady Enies, the Former Vice Captain, and Lady Sakura, the previous Rank Nine who fought for her Captain's word, and thus entered into the Rank of Two.

After they had used the mysterious Teleportation Chambers that returned them to the base of Force Tower, the three sisters had headed towards the Central Tower where they split up and went into their sleeping chambers. Maile soon found she was too scared to sleep in her room alone, and returned to Remi's room for the night. Baelie, who was more than excited, had dashed away to her own room in preparation for their so-called 'S Rank Mission.' Although Remi kept sarcastically hinting that there was no possible way they would have been given such a high-ranking mission, she was secretly hoping beyond anything else that it truly was not an S ranking mission. When she thought of it too much, her heart started to race and dark thoughts came into her mind.

Remi tried to clear her head after returning to her room, only acknowledging the warmth of her blankets and the softness of her pillows. She dreamt of adorable little Tree Spirits, which looked like flying kittens wrapped in snow; their soft black ears, big blue eyes and little wings. She wished more than anything that she could keep one forever, yet as soon as she had successfully stolen one back in her dreams, the daunting form of a blood-soaked Lady Enies had risen from the ground, and her eyes had snapped open. That had been her wakeup call.

In the morning, the waning Sun peeked through the blinds, casting a fallow glow over her room. She laid in bed for a few moments, reminiscing over the day before and the terrifying powers of the Force Corps. She had never seen anything like them. They were truly like warriors from another realm. The way they moved … the way they could fly … their power and agility. Everything seemed like a fairy tale coming to life. A nervousness much like what she felt when going to the Valyti came over her as she thought of their mission; a mission given to them by the greatest fighter of their world: Lady Scylla the Valiant.

After a few minutes, she rose from bed and walked to the nearby window and opened it. The cold morning air sent her rushing back to the warmth under her heavy fur blankets, but not before she saw black clouds rolling atop the rising Sun. A strong gust slammed the window shut, leaving her startled.

Lying in bed, Remi looked around her room. It wasn't the largest of sleeping chambers, but it was comfortable. She lay in a huge bed, staring up at the walls. Each was lined with dozens and dozens of books upon shelves—she had read all of them. It looked as if a hurricane had struck her closet; clothes dangled from chairs, from her desk, and off the sides of her bed. She sighed, dreading the time she would have to spend cleaning. She didn't understand how her room got so messy, being that she could have sworn she just cleaned it. On the far end of room, meticulously placed on the side of the longest wall, was a wall-scroll of the rock band Rose's Echo. They were her favorite band in all of Soria, along with almost every other teenager. She sighed, wondering if she would ever get the chance to see them in concert. On the other side of her bed was little Maile, sleeping silently with her helmet clutched lazily in her arms. She smiled, realizing that her little sister was probably the cutest thing she knew. Well, maybe with the exception of the little Tree Spirits.

After making sure Maile was sleeping soundly, Remi reached to the side of her bed and clicked a hidden button. A sliver of wood slid out from the side of her bed: upon it was a faded black book with sleek silver runes etched upon the cover—'*Remi's Journal*'. She took the little black book and a feathered pen from her bedside table. She began to flip through the pages, seeking one untarnished by her ink. It wasn't until she had flipped to the very last page that she found one. One last remaining page.

I can't believe I'm on the last page, she thought. *It feels like I just started writing this yesterday.* Sadness overtook her as she remembered the first day she started writing in her journal. It had been a gift from her parents and she remembered thinking that a journal was the worst kind of present. At first she hadn't written in it at all, not until she realized they weren't coming back. From then on, she always wrote her memories down so she would never forget the past, as she now knew that things just have a way of quickly disappearing. She ran her fingers over the hard leather of the book; it was the last present she had ever been given by her parents—her final memory of them.

She flipped back through the pages and stopped on the very first page she had ever written. It was still perfectly flat and clean. At the very top of the page were black runes written in her own perfect handwriting.

"*The Promise,*" she said softly, and began to read.

Dear Stupid Little Book,

I became an orphan today. This morning was when we first heard … My sisters are too young to really understand what happened, but

I know. I don't know why, but I had this feeling yesterday that they shouldn't leave, not that it would have made a difference ... not with Break. Officials appeared at our house this morning, and even though they wouldn't tell us what was wrong, or where our mom and dad were, we knew something bad had happened.

Our parents didn't come home the night before and now Officials were visiting our home in their stead. As soon as they said the word Break I knew, but I couldn't believe it. I wouldn't believe it. The rarest disease in all of Soria. No one knew why or how it happened. Just that it did. And when it did, there was no waking up. They tried to console us, tell us everything was going to be alright. How do you tell someone that everything is going to be alright the moment their life completely changes?

Maile couldn't stop crying, even before they told us. It was as if she already knew. Like a small piece of her soul had disappeared and she could feel it gone. Baelie ... Well, she's been quiet since then and hasn't spoken much. I saw it in her eyes, the pain, and I know that she feels this is her fault. Our parents always gave Baelie a hard time because of her weight. I hope she doesn't feel they didn't love her as much as Maile and me. And more than anything I hope that is not the truth ...

After their ideas lid to success, our lives had changed so much, so fast, that we could hardly keep up ... But the worst thing of all was that they'd changed. They stopped tucking Maile in at night, and we would just wait up until neither of us could keep our eyes open anymore before they came home. Baelie seemed to cope by eating, as she has always loved to eat, and because of that, our parents started to outcast her in ways. It was something they had never done before, but after we moved to the bigger house, they made new friends—friends who made them act different when they were around us. Even though Maile and I were treated the same, Baelie would sometimes get locked in her room ... punishments for things she hadn't done, or didn't understand. They didn't know that she cried every night before she slept, wondering why it was that she couldn't be like everyone else.

I thought I was happy before this happened. I thought that I had all my parent's love; that I was their golden child. At the Academy, where I am a Sixth Ring student, everyone knows who I am and thinks I am pretty. Especially after we'd moved, everyone wanted to be my friend. We used to make fun of the 'Others': the ones with Broken Families, or the ones whose parents had been inflicted with Break. They disgusted me and I felt that if I was beside them, I would also become Broken. That's why they have no friends. That's why no one likes them. They are alone in this world. And now, so am I.

She flipped to the next journal entry marked for a few days later …

Today was the first day I realized how cruel I have been. I went to the Academy this morning and it was so weird. It was as if everyone had already known what happened before I even did. I waved at my friends but they lowered their eyes and walked in the opposite direction, as if they were scared of me. I tried to follow them and ask what happened, but Ophelia turned around abruptly and called me "disgusting," and said that I was now one of the "Others." They left me in the empty courtyard with tears as my only comfort. That day was the first time I ever sat alone at lunch, underneath the golden apple tree in the corner of the courtyard. I remember looking at the apples and wondering if they felt the pain of death after falling from their tree … I sat for so long I didn't know if I would just wither into the ground. I could not go home. I could not eat, but then I saw them walking towards me. My group of friends that is, and I was happy that they would finally talk to me.

I wiped my tears and looked up smiling.

It wasn't the first time I had been wrong about something.

They told me not to come back to the Academy. That now that my parents were Broken, my family had become nothing. I had become nothing. My parent's disease had corrupted my entire being, and I was no longer one of them. They told me that one day I would fall under Break, and no one would ever remember me ever again. I had already cried enough tears and fought back, and even though I was strong, Ophelia's older brother kicked me down. He kicked dirt in my eyes and pulled my hair, and all I wanted to do was disappear and never come back again. All I wanted was to die. I didn't even care if I fell into Break.

And then I heard him yell.

"Leave her alone!" I heard but I couldn't open my eyes.

I don't even know if I could, or maybe … I just didn't want to. I didn't want to be saved, yet I did. I felt as if I was being ripped apart in two different directions … I didn't recognize the voice until they spoke his name, and I couldn't believe it, but even then I still didn't open my eyes.

"If it isn't poor little Ladon," they said. "The 'Others' are going to protect each other now? No one likes you. No one will ever like you. You will never have friends and you are disgusting!"

I knew the name, and the strangely accented voice after hearing it. Ladon's mother had been inflicted with Break the past cycle. Even before it happened he didn't have any friends, but after, everything was much worse for him. I used to make fun of him every day, pretend to sit next to him, just to see him smile before laughing and watching my friends throw things at him from hidden places. I didn't understand why he was protecting me now. After everything I did, why did he protect me? Why? The taste of my tears … I'll never forget it. Not at that moment.

"Leave her alone," he said again.

I dared not open my eyes, but my ears could not deceive me. Ophelia's brother was an Eighth Ring and Ladon was even smaller than me. I could hear them beating him, his lurching coughs and painful breaths, yet I still did not open my eyes. But he never ran away … Why didn't he run away!? I lay there long after they left, until Ladon finally sat up and asked if I was hurt. I didn't answer him and he didn't speak again. I heard him walk away, but it wasn't graceful and I knew he was limping. I tried to cry but I couldn't. My tears were dried up. I had nothing left to live for. I hated everyone. Why did my life turn out like this? It wasn't supposed to be like this!

It was dark and cold before I moved. When I opened my eyes, I could taste the salt from my tears in my mouth. My arms hurt really badly, like I had been hit with a club. I stumbled around dizzily, not knowing where I wanted to go, or what to do, and like this I wandered for I don't know how long.

At some point I heard a strange clicking sound. Turning my head, I wearily opened my eyes to see a playground surrounded by tall trees. And there, sitting in the middle of it was little blond-haired Ladon.

His cuts and bruises were not bandaged, but there he was playing with something and speaking to himself. I walked closer. Neither of us said anything for a long time but I knew he was aware of my presence. Finally, I broke the silence.

"What are you doing here?"

"Are you ok?" *were his first words. I was taken aback. It only made me madder that he still cared, after I proved so many times that I cared so little about him.*

"Why do you care!?" *I shouted.* "I hated you all this time for what you are, so why show me kindness now!?"

"Because I know what it feels like … to be hated by everybody."

I didn't speak. I couldn't speak. I knew that whatever I felt, he had felt for a long time, much longer than I had. I watched him turn his head and look at the stars, and without thinking, maybe because he and I were of the same kind now, I sat down beside him, and my anger left me slowly. Despite my sadness, it was in that moment that I felt comforted for the first time since it happened.

"I just … want them back," *I said, trying to hold back my tears. It didn't work. As soon as the first tear fell, they rained until I was sobbing uncontrollably. It was then that I felt him embrace me, and it reminded me of what my father would have done when I cried. I froze when I felt his small bruised arms surround me, but when I looked into his eyes, I understood him completely. It was then that I saw him for the first time. He knew what I wanted, because he himself had been wanting it for so long. He may have been younger than me, but for some reason he felt much older …*

It felt like many shades that we sat together and I cried until my cheeks grew dry and all I could do was breathe softly. I will never forget the words he spoke next.

"Don't worry …" *he said,* "I'm going to cure them … I'm going to cure the disease Break. I'm going to save my mother."

I shook my head. "That's impossible. It's not curable! They said those with Break are taken to Starseeker, the Tower of the Damned! There they will spend all of eternity sleeping, never to wake again."

"Anything's curable," *he said confidently, and I could tell he was smiling again.* "As long as you never give up, ever. And if what you're fighting for is something close to your heart, I don't think *giving up is really ever an option." He ran to the ladder and climbed it. "Come on" he said holding out his hand, and without thinking, I took it. We stood next to each other at the top of the playground. The stars were so bright that night, as if his voice brought them life, or maybe it was their light that was strengthening his voice.*

"You know why they named it Starseeker, right?" he asked. I shook my head.` "They say that those sleeping can only find what they seek in the stars … as if their remedy lies within them."

"You really think —"

But he interrupted. "My da and I have been working on a cure since my mother …" He suppressed the pain in his voice, swallowing hard. "I'll never give up no matter what. My da and I, we're genius inventors! Even if I have to fly to the moon, even if I have to harness the power of the stars, even if I have to win the Soldier Games … I'll do it. Anything."

I smiled for the first time. And then impulsively, I stood up and looked Ladon in the eyes. I spoke without thinking. "Then promise me something."

"I promise," he said, smiling back at me.

"But I didn't say anything yet."

"It doesn't matter. I promise." His eyes flashed bright blue and a grin curved from ear to ear. It was then, that after all I had lost, I felt that I had actually found something … Something I could believe in. It was a feeling that surged through my body like life rekindled, like I had finally found a reason to keep moving forward.

Something strange happened then. It was as if the light of the stars were showing me a different boy than the one I had always seen. I had never cared to talk to him before, yet even after so much torment and pain, he could still smile, he could still make promises, and even though I was the last one in the world that he should make a promise to … he did. He suddenly seemed so strong, so brave, and so full of integrity. I felt like the rest of the night was a dream, and I couldn't stop this weird feeling I had every time I looked at him. Something about his intensity, something about the strength in his words, it was as if he knew that there was nothing that could stop him, as if no matter what happened, he would find a cure. Against all odds, against all the times of Soria, and all those who would call him crazy, against

the Incurable Disease known as Break—the disease that could cast
any of us into an endless sleep, a sleep from which none have ever
awoken. He would defeat it, and I believed in him.

It was tonight that I knew you were the one, Ladon …

And I will think of you every night until I die …

A sudden knock at the door shook Remi's concentration. Looking up, she found herself staring into the eyes of Maile, who had woken and was peering at her from under the blankets.

"Remi," she whispered. "Why are you crying?"

Remi rubbed her eyes and forced a smile. "I'm not! I just had something stuck in my eye." Just then the door flung open, and there, standing in the doorway was a thick figure with her hands placed on her hips; from her back was a cloak that billowed out behind her. The dark silhouette soon came into light, and Remi's eyes fell on her sister Baelie, who entered the room.

"What are you doing in bed still!?" she cried. "I barely slept a wink last night. Today's the day we take up our first S Class mission for the Force Corps!" She stopped suddenly. "Are you crying!?"

Remi shook her head, trying not to laugh.

Baelie grinned and gave her a double thumbs-up. "Don't worry Big Rem, I'll protect you."

Remi's eyes grew sharp as daggers. "What did you just call me?" In a flash, Remi seized one of her pillows and chucked it through the air. Baelie moved just out of the way, and as the pillow flew past her, another figure entered the room. The pillow greeted her straight in the face.

"Lady Arya!" cried Baelie, turning and pointing at Remi. "It was Remi! She's the culprit!"

Remi froze and Maile disappeared under the blankets. The pillow slid down Lady Arya's face as if in slow motion, revealing her dark skin and the Number *4* etched into her shoulder. A split second later, the pillow exploded into a thousand feathers.

"Ahhhhh!!!! My pillow!" screamed Remi. She gulped

as her eyes met Lady Arya's; they were like cold, hard ice, piercing towards her own.

"Don't even think about it," seethed Lady Arya. "Now get ready. We leave in five minutes. I'll be escorting you to your post, where you will remain throughout the day. The *whole* day."

"Five minutes!?" squealed Remi. "I need at least two hours!"

"Told you," said Baelie, holding out her hand. Lady Arya's raised an eyebrow as she pulled one golden sori from a leather pouch at her side and dropped it into Baelie's hand.

"I told you she's ridiculous," said Baelie, grinning. "Thinks she's a princess or something."

Lady Arya pursed her lips then sighed. "Might as well be … five minutes!"

The door shut.

Remi shook her fist at the door before turning around. There, lying on her fur blankets was her faded black journal. The sorrow that had earlier engulfed her returned. She reached down to the secret button and placed the journal back in its hiding spot.

Whatever happened to you, Ladon?

Why did you disappear after that night? After you promised me …

I just wish I knew where you were … and why you left …

Many thoughts ran through her mind swiftly, leaving her no consolation. She looked to the window and wondered why the boy who had changed her so greatly had disappeared. Maybe he had given up? Maybe it really was impossible to cure Break. She shook her head and looked towards her closet. She didn't want to believe or think anything like that. He was still alive. He was still working towards curing Break. He had to be.

"C'mon Remi," nudged Maile. "I think Lady Arya was serious about the five minute thing …"

"Five minutes my —" Remi started.

The door blasted open, "Remi! You only have three

minutes left!" boomed Baelie.

That morning pillows soared across Remi's chambers like a flock of spooked willows.

XL – Storm's Fear?

Caim and Storm walked in wonder up the stone bridge that carved through the sky. Storm could feel everything he knew fading away behind him. Only uncertainty awaited them. The deathly warnings of the Soldier Games traced through his thoughts.

"This is *the* bridge … the one that connects the two worlds!" said Caim, distracting him. In a sense, he was happy he did.

The bridge was carved of perfectly black stone, without a blemish or scratch visible from any angle; the width of the bridge stretched out nearly the width of the entire city of Trestles. Caim could not see from one end to the other. A great coliseum rose in the distance, stretching up and into the dark clouds of the sky like the rising of a King's Crown.

Caim spread his arms wide, "it's huge!! That's where the tournament is!"

"How do you know?" asked Storm.

"I overheard someone talking about yesterday," said Caim. "I wonder what kind of strong fighters we'll meet in there … I bet they're even stronger than grandpa!"

Storm flinched at Caim's mentioning of their grandfather. Remnants of the dream were still lingering in his thoughts.

"Doubtful," said Storm. He couldn't imagine someone being stronger than the old man. In all his days, he had never met someone who was even a fraction of his strength. He looked up at the coliseum in the distance.

"I wonder what it looks like inside," said Storm, but Caim was already running towards the outer wall that rose up along the edge of the bridge. Before Storm could say anything, Caim jumped swiftly up the twenty or thirty feet and landed on the top.

He shouted down. "Storm! This is crazy! Come check this out! I can see the entire world! I can see the bottoms of Falia and Risia! There's a whole bunch of weird green vines and leaves hanging down!"

Storm turned back to see Caim staring over the edge of the wall, and with a great reluctance, walked forward until he was at the base of the high side-wall.

Guess it's so no one falls off, he thought, staring at it. He jumped up and landed next to his brother.

Storm felt his stomach turn and his heart race as he stared over the edge. Beneath him was nothing but wispy clouds racing through the air. It was as if the bridge was swaying over the sky above, and he suddenly had the feeling that it was leaning back and forth. He pulled himself back from the edge quietly.

Caim eyed Storm suspiciously, "What's up with you? You scared?"

Storm took a deep breath and scrubbed his sweaty palms on his pants. "Caim, don't be stupid." He tried to seem confident, but his racing heart betrayed his words.

Caim smirked. "Then come stand over here like this." Caim walked to the very edge of the railing and turned his back to the open sky, lifting his arms to his sides.

"Caim, stop being an idiot!" said Storm. "We have to hurry. Don't you remember they said everyone was already gathering at the base of the ... whatever you call it."

Caim's eyes grew wide in astonishment. "You are, aren't you!?" Suddenly Caim's foot slipped and he fell backwards, straight off the side of the wall, vanishing into the empty sky. Storm heard him scream on the way down.

"YOU IDIOT!" cried Storm. He dashed forward, but balked at the side. His panic, however, was short-lived, for just over the side of the bridge and floating in the air was Caim, clutching his stomach and laughing hysterically.

"How can you be scared of heights when you can fly!?" cried Caim.

"I hate you," said Storm under his breath. He immediately turned from the wall and jumped back down to the black stone pathway. Turning his gaze towards the rising coliseum in the distance, he continued walking. In the meantime, Caim had not finished having fun, and slowly but surely, crept forward through the air, floating with his arms and legs crossed while making little turns and flips.

"Stop doing that," said Storm.

Caim continued floating above Storm's head and pretended to stroke an imaginary beard. He spoke in the stentorian tones of their grandfather. "Hmm, why Storm, now that I think about it, I've never actually seen you fly outside of Inner Deep, ka ..."

Storm's eyes narrowed. "It's *Inner Depths*. And what exactly are you trying to say, Caim?"

Caim continued stroking his imaginary beard. "Well maybe you're scared of heights because you can't fly ... ka." A grin curved across his face.

Storm quickly turned to Caim. "I CAN FLY, Caim!" He punched upwards in the air.

"I don't think so," said Caim, darting away from Storm's fist. Caim floated a good ten feet above Storm, taunting him and singing, "You're as skillful as a stone ... " Caim had two fingers held together as he was doing his little dance in the air and wasn't paying attention when Storm's foot cracked into the ground of the bridge. Suddenly, Caim was staring eye to eye with Storm, who was floating before him.

"Guess it's too late to apologize then?"

"Yep," answered Storm, "too late." Caim gulped and felt Storm grab his ankle and spin him round and round before he was catapulted to the black stone below.

"Ahhhh, I'm sorry!!" yelled Caim as he crashed. Storm landed with a *tmp* at his side. Caim stared up at him with spinning eyes.

"Told you I could fly." Caim's eyes were still spinning and he felt like he could see three or four Storms standing above him. He then saw three or four Storms walk away. After the spinning calmed down, Caim stood and wobbled after Storm.

"You only jumped," said Caim under his breath. Storm ignored him and kept walking.

As they proceeded up the bridge, bright lights and colored tents started to come into view. Soon they could hear the rumbling beat of drums and the smell of exotic foods. Caim's mouth began to water as they made their way closer, and they began to walk a little bit faster, both of them getting a little more excited with each step.

They soon came upon rows and rows of tents along the bridge wall. Behind each were large open areas laden with hundreds of trinkets of different shapes and sizes. Storm noticed that behind each of the tents, on both sides of the bridge, were statues of warriors wearing grand cloaks and wielding ancient weapons. There were even statues of Kushala Flares, Raelics, Chameleoths, and many other creatures Storm had never laid eyes upon. He noticed that the farther they walked along the bridge, the bigger the statues grew in size, as if they were leading him towards the coliseum.

Caim pointed at one, "look it's Galfungyon!"

Storm sighed and then smiled. He thought back to the great creature from two nights before. "Seriously neo, you have to work on your names."

"There must be a lot of Sorians who come to this tournament," said Caim, looking around.

"The old man said everyone on Soria watches the games."

Caim scratched his head. "I wonder how many that is."

"More than you can count, that's for sure."

Carts of meats and vegetables and desserts were lined along the walls, while crafts, weapons, armor, alchemy shops and other things the boys couldn't recognize opened up before them. The crowd of Sorians on the bridge grew thicker and thicker as they inched their way forward. Caim's eyes spent a large amount of time surveying a tent with hundreds of shimmering silver blades hanging from within its canvas walls.

"Come on Caim," Storm said several times as they passed the festivities.

The tents stretched on for quite a while, and as they moved, the size of the coliseum became clear. Even from afar it looked enormous, but when coming upon the base of it, they felt as if they were staring up at a huge mountain that had grown out of white stone. Its shadow seemed to engulf the world. Storm leaned his head back and looked up.

"Wow," he whispered. He felt a cool breeze brush past him, and a shiver ran through his bones. Turning his eyes back down, he noticed something he hadn't before.

Something about the coliseum wasn't right. Lurking around its sides was a strange change in the air, a sort of shimmering that prevented him from seeing its true features. It puzzled him. They soon came upon a colossal set of stairs carved into the statue of a dragon. They tried to follow the stairs up with their eyes; it wound up and into the sky, yet the peak of them was clouded from their sight.

"Do we go up?" asked Caim.

"I don't think so," said Storm. "The guards said something about meeting at the base of it." He looked forward into the gloomy darkness past the stairs. The prospect was becoming more and more daunting. A feeling of anxiety had been growing within him as he walked.

"Let's walk this way," said Storm, pointing into the darkness.

"But I wanna see what's at the top," whined Caim. Storm waved his hand over his head and started walking away. Caim looked to the top of the coliseum. Then he looked at Storm. Then back to the top. And back to Storm. Frustrated, he sighed and followed Storm into the curious mist.

"Why is it so misty around this place?"

"How am I supposed to know?" answered Storm. *"Everything about this coliseum is confusing."* He didn't even want to start thinking about how such a massive coliseum could be supported by this bridge. Nothing about it made any sense.

The farther they walked from the rising staircase, the more the air became damp and misty, and soon there was little each of them could see in either direction. It was as if a moat of swirling thick fog rotated and clung to the lower base of the coliseum. Even the black stone at their feet grew faint before them.

Storm had been silent as they passed through the shadows, and had closed his eyes many long minutes before, guiding himself with only the feel of aura around him. Before him stretched a dark world, pierced by tiny pricks of light, each representing the life force of a Sorian. Like this, Storm could sense everything around him; from the lifeless objects of swords and shields, to the different assortment of foods in the tents they had passed; even the sounds that waved through the empty space left remnant trails of seeping aura. This was a skill at which Storm was much more adept than Caim. It was one that required focusing all of one's mind on something very vague—seeing all that lies within and around. As they neared the dark base of the coliseum, Storm's mind twitched, as if a foreign force were approaching, and much brighter lights came to be in his dark world. There were dozens of them, or more, and they were all gathered not too far ahead; at the base of the coliseum he guessed, which rose like a veil of shadows in his mind.

It was then that Storm felt them. He stopped abruptly. Huge powers were not far from them. *These must be the contestants,* thought Storm. Their aura levels were much higher than the Nobles they'd encountered in the restaurant. His heart started to race. He shook off the excitement and focused. They would come across the fighters soon. His fingers fell on the hilt of his katana. He suddenly had a bad feeling that the armor and keys wouldn't be nearly enough.

His thoughts began to grow violent, thinking of what would happen if they were caught. Curseborn infiltrating the Soldier Games, surrounded by Nobles. And they were severely outnumbered. There was no way the two of them would be able to fight them off, or even flee. He tried to swallow but his mouth was too dry. At the very least, it would prove to be the greatest fight of his life, even if the outcome was Death. He found himself smiling at the prospect of such a fight, despite his fear.

Just as he was about to open his eyes, a sudden burning light seared his senses and he turned, reluctantly northward, toward the rising castle in the distance. He felt like his mind was being sucked towards it and there was nothing he could do about it. He was flying, mentally, faster than ever, until he was upon it and stopped. There, within the walls of the great White Castle were several tremendous lights, each glowing with the power and fury of a star; and Storm was cast into a state of shock by their presence.

Why can't I control myself!? His thoughts were screaming as he tried to regain control of his senses.

He focused harder and pushed his feeling outward, trying to find the source of the one that had burned his senses until within the very core of the castle, two separate lights, each with the power of a Sun, captured him. He suddenly felt as if he couldn't breathe; as if he were weighed down underwater, struggling to break the surface. And then, just like that, one of the Suns turned its light in his direction, glowing brighter and brighter with blinding strife until …

"Storm?" asked Caim, placing his hand on his shoulder. Storm's eyes snapped open. Life surged back into his body and it took all his power not to collapse to the floor. A trickle of sweat ran down his forehead, down his nose and dripped off.

"What is it?" asked Caim. "You look sick."

"Caim …" Storm spoke through heavy breaths as he tried to collect himself. "You were right."

"Right about what?"

Storm struggled to control himself. Just when Caim thought he might collapse from his shaking, he stood tall, and his eyes lit up like a Flare sensing blood.

"There *are* those stronger than the old man."

XLI – The Relic Room

Twenty-five minutes later Remi walked out of the door, sparkling like she just waltzed out of a picture frame. She wore her favorite brown leather jacket over a white shirt and skirt. She held in her hand another copy of her favorite book. Maile followed with her elbow pads, kneepads, and helmet, equipped and ready, and Baelie was standing out of the doorway, secretly admiring Lady Arya from a distance.

"Can't imagine you could have gone any faster?" asked Lady Arya.

"That was fast!" said Remi proudly. "I think that's a new record."

Baelie held out her hand again, "Told you. I really should do this for a living." Lady Arya's mouth hung open again, and even more reluctantly than the first time, dropped Baelie another golden sori.

Lady Arya turned down the hallway and then froze. Almost instantaneously, she kneeled and bowed her head. Baelie was taken aback, wondering why Lady Arya was suddenly bowing to her. And then she heard it, echoing from down the hall. It was the echo of silver heels.

"My Captain," said Lady Arya. "You've come."

Remi turned very slowly and Maile tried to disguise herself next to the wall of the corridor. Walking towards them was none other than the Lady Scylla, her brilliant silver armor flashing with each step, her cloak flowing softly in her wake.

"I can't believe this," muttered Remi in utter awe. She had never seen Lady Scylla this close. Baelie stood frozen, unable to move, unable to think. She felt she might collapse from pure elation.

"Lady Arya," Lady Scylla gently. "I thank you for coming to accompany these three to the Relic Room, but I will take it from here."

Arya bowed her head. "Surely you have more important matters to attend to, my Captain. I assure you it is really no issue at all."

Lady Scylla raised her hand. "It is quite alright. This is the mission I have chosen for them and it is only right that I accompany them myself, especially after the mess in the Valyti. And not just that but …" She gazed to Baelie and placed her hand on her shoulder. "I have received dozens of letters from this little one. I believe she has very much wanted to meet me for some time now." She looked Baelie in the eye.

Baelie couldn't move. She couldn't breathe. Her childhood hero was standing before her, acknowledging her. *Her.* It was a dream come true. She wanted to cry, to scream, but with all her might she forced her hand into a Sorian salute and kneeled. "Lady Scylla the Valiant … I am at your command!"

Dozens of letters? Remi half smiled as she realized that maybe all the nights Baelie had been sneaking into the kitchens she might have been using the food to stay awake and write letters. She turned to Lady Scylla and gave the salute.

"Please Baelie," said Lady Scylla, taking Baelie's hand gently. "Such formalities are not required when speaking with me."

Baelie's eyes widened.

Arya finally spoke, "Very well, my Captain, I will take

my leave." Lady Scylla nodded. Arya turned away and walked back down the hallway from which Lady Scylla had come.

"First things first," spoke Lady Scylla. She turned to look at Remi and then Maile. "I would like to apologize for the heinous actions of Lady Enies during your visit to the Valyti. If I had predicted such an outcome, I would have come and delivered the message personally." She lowered her eyes and bowed. "My sincerest apologies. Children of your age should not bear witness to such evil behavior. And know now that such behavior is not to be tolerated within my lands. Justice is what we know, not crude conduct and outright disrespect."

"It's … quite alright," answered Baelie, adopting Lady Scylla's use of the word "quite," and trying to mimic her tone and confidence. Remi could tell Baelie didn't know how to react. The greatest hero of their world was kneeling and apologizing to her. The whole situation seemed as if it were a lopsided dream.

"This is your first mission," Lady Scylla spoke. "Now then," she continued, standing. "As you have been told. You three have been assigned an S Rank mission. It is known as the guarding of the Relic Room. For ages past, this castle has never been breached, and for all those ages, we have guarded the treasures of the Relic Room as if it were itself, the castle. Each cycle, the guarding of the door is switched off between the Force and the Shield, and although the ranked one through nine soldiers do not guard the door, the lower level tiers of soldiers are always stationed to defend it."

"Don't you think we are a bit unqualified?" asked Remi, feeling somewhat confused. As Lady Scylla glanced up at her, Remi realized that one of her eyes was a soft pale grey with no color. Remi shivered, remembering that she often saw the young captain of the Force wearing an eyepatch.

"On the contrary, young ones, Baelie has proven to me through her many letters the dedication and loyalty she bears to the Empress and the Force. I believe she has more of what it takes to be a great soldier than many might believe: passion being one of them. Always remember that passion is the root of all things great. And for you two, her sisters. It is you who will be the voice of reason, the support that allows young Baelie to keep fighting for her dreams. This is the sole purpose for which I have chosen the three of you."

She turned to Baelie. "I'm entrusting you with a very important mission, Baelie." She stole a glance at her tree branch spear. "That's a fine spear you have crafted," she said with a genuine smile. Baelie beamed proudly, and a single tear glistened down her cheek.

"Perhaps if the mission goes according to plan, I can arrange for a new spear to be crafted for you." Baelie blinked in sheer disbelief. The day was becoming greater and greater by the second.

Baelie saluted firmly. "Thank you, Lady Scylla the Valia—Lady Scylla. We will not let you down!"

"I believe that you won't."

Remi stared at her curiously. She never would have expected someone of her caliber to act as she was. She would have thought that such a great hero might have an air of superiority, or act much more like Lady Enies in the presence of Baelie, but she didn't. She was humble and calm and kind. A new respect for the Captain of the Force was born in Remi, and for the first moment since they had heard of the mission, she didn't feel so wary about it.

Baelie snapped to attention, "Big Rem, Lil Mai! Line up, you're my backup on this mission!"

Remi smirked and walked past her sister, "don't get ahead of yourself dreamer child." Baelie scowled at Remi as she passed. Remi snickered as she knew Baelie didn't want to look undermined in front of her hero.

"So … what's the Relic Room?" asked Remi.

Lady Scylla turned, her gaze becoming serious. "The Relic Room is a room of treasures that Soria has accumulated over all of the past ages. Many ancient artifacts lie in that room, artifacts that hold great and also unknown powers. But do not fear, the castle cannot be breached. Although you protect the door, there can be none who reach it. However, those who have seen much might say that such treasures unlock the greed in those weak of heart. We guard the door, not to protect against those who might strike from the outside, but from those who realize the power in what lies so close to them."

Power? Thought Remi, unsure as to why she would have chosen that word over value. *She acts as if there is something else in this room other than just treasures ...*

"You think the door might be breached by someone inside the castle?" asked Baelie.

Lady Scylla held a solemn expression. "I only understand that in possibility lies risk. And only when one assumes the possibility to be none, do such things prove themselves possible. The protection of the castle, the Empress, and Soria are my objectives, with which I take extreme care and caution. The door will always be guarded, and therefore will never be breached."

"I see ..." answered Remi. "This is about preventing anything that *could* happen."

"Exactly, little one. And it might just be that all three of you have a place in the Force in your later rings."

Remi felt her cheeks warm, but not in a good way. "I actually ... well, thank you." She felt it would be rude to blatantly tell Lady Scylla that she had no interest in joining the Force whatsoever. She looked to Baelie who was saluting so fiercely her entire body was quivering.

Lady Scylla turned her back to them. "Come then, I will escort you three to the Relic Room. We haven't much time. I am to meet with Lord Falkor, Captain of the Shield, and his *pet* Vasuki."

Did she just refer to the Vice Captain of the Shield as Lord Falkor's pet? Remi couldn't help but smile at the thought. She had always thought of Vasuki as a terrifying creature, most likely raised in the darkness of Mortal Aeryx.

Baelie's eyes lit up, "You're escorting the Empress to the Soldier Games?"

Lady Scylla started walking away. "One such as myself

has many responsibilities, young Baelie. And now just as I do, you three also have a responsibility. Come, let us be on our way."

Baelie immediately fell in step behind her. Lady Scylla was personally coming to escort them to the Relic Room, just before she was going to escort the Empress. What she was doing was more than a kind deed. It was the kindest anyone had been to her in longer than she could remember. It was an act Baelie would remember for the rest of her life.

Baelie bowed her head deeply and spoke in the strongest voice she could muster. "Thank you so much, Lady Scylla the Valiant!" She decided to regard her in the utmost formality, for that was how she viewed her. Then, gripping her branch spear tightly, she clattered down the long hallway in her kitchenware armor as her two sisters followed closely behind.

It wasn't long before they had reached the end of the corridor and started traveling up a twisting staircase. Remi, who had been curious about the Relic Room, finally asked the question that had been bothering her.

"So you really don't know what's in the Relic Room?"

"I know of a few things," Lady Scylla said after a pause, "but for the vast majority of its contents, I am left in the dark. I prefer it that way. Temptation can be a dangerous foe to even the strongest will."

Remi sighed. She had been hoping for a lengthy story about a trinket, or anything that might reveal the secret about the power hidden with the room.

Maile reached up and pulled on her sleeve. "I bet it has lots of amazing treasure in it!" She often dreamed of finding treasure chests in secret places.

"Don't even think about it," said Lady Scylla. She smiled, but her back was turned and the three of them could not see. "If one were to enter the Relic Room without the correct precautions, one would surely …"

"Surely?" said Remi and Maile in unison.

"Surely …" said Lady Scylla.

"Surely?" Remi and Maile again echoed, clutching each other's hands.

"Die."

A loud shriek echoed down the staircase and into the

corridors. Many of the guards standing on floors above and below tightened their grip on their weapons. For the remainder of the walk, Remi and Maile followed with pale faces, imagining the horrors of the room. They soon made their way to the center of the tower and found a Ring Lift, which they used to ascend to the higher levels. They had only been up this high a few times, and it wasn't often that they were allowed.

They stopped on a high floor, and Remi and Maile froze at the overwhelming darkness. There were no lights and no window. Only a few dimly lit lanterns led the way down a winding corridor that gave them the feeling of walking into a snake mouth. Shivers ran down their spines as they thought of all the terrors and booby traps that might await them. Lady Scylla led the way swiftly and it wasn't long before they were staring up at a massive wooden door lined with black stone and inscribed with many silver runes running up its sides.

"This is the Relic Room," said Lady Scylla. "Don't move from your post. Don't eat. Don't breathe. I wish you the best. May the light of Vale shine upon you."

"But we'll die if we don't breathe!" whimpered Maile, trying to hold her breath.

"I think she's kidding," said Remi, but Lady Scylla's glance was stern.

At that moment a chaotic feeling engulfed the four of them—it was as if some foreign pressure were squeezing and forcing the life out of them. The very life force of the castle seemed to be pressing in against them from all angles. Remi fell to her knees and her head began to spin. Maile had collapsed to her knees beside her, and Baelie beside her. She choked trying to speak but couldn't. Her heart began to beat rapidly upon realizing that she was having great trouble breathing. She looked up at Lady Scylla in despair who was standing completely still, her focused eyes looking eastward. And then, just like that the feeling vanished.

The three girls gasped for air. Lady Scylla's face hadn't changed in the slightest. Under her breath Remi heard her say something along the lines of, "Looks like Grahf's prison chambers need to be recharged."

"What was that?" asked Maile, trying not to cry.

"Don't ask questions about things that do not concern you. There are things of this world that you would not believe even were you told by me. Now, remember your task, girls," said Lady Scylla, and walked down the hall.

"Remi ..." whispered Maile, "I'm scared. What was that?"

"I don't know but I've never felt something like that before," answered Remi, wearily standing to her feet. Remi only knew one thing about what had just happened. It was dangerous. The feeling was not natural. It had felt as dark as a night with no moon.

Silence engulfed them as they thought. Baelie, who had turned and was staring up at the massive door, finally spoke. Swinging her branch spear out to her side, she slammed its point to the stone, causing a loud *crack*.

"I don't know what the hell that was, but this is awesome! I'll be the Vice Captain in no time!"

XLII – The Opening Acts

*S*torm struggled to catch his breath. What he had just felt was a power beyond anything he had ever experienced. Caim's eyes were bright and gazing toward where the aura had come from.

"Holy shit," said Caim. "I don't know what that was, but I hope it's one of the fighters in the tournament. That's insane!"

Storm took a second to regain his composure. A smile came over his face.

"An opponent that could give me a cold sweat from leagues away," said Storm. "Now I know this tournament was worth sneaking into." Caim smacked his fist into his hand in acknowledgement.

For a moment the two brothers stood still, feeling the other distant powers and preparing themselves mentally for what was to come. Everything their old man had told them was turning out to be true. Yet, something was bothering Storm. The one extremely powerful aura was far different than the rest, and he couldn't help but wonder who it could have been, or what.

XLII – THE OPENING ACTS

Storm started walking ahead of his brother and for a few long minutes, neither of them spoke. What had he felt from the castle? Could that have really been a Sorian? The power was beyond anything he even thought was possible, or existed. He clenched his fist, wondering just what the two of them had gotten themselves into. Finally lifting his eyes toward the distance, he found that they were coming upon a group of soldiers.

They soldiers stood at the base of the coliseum, exactly as the guard had said. Flickers of sunlight pierced through the heavy mist and illuminated the sides of the enormous walls. This was it. They were actually doing it. He could see the shine of their silver armor glinting in the distance. There were dozens, no, more than dozens. Over a hundred Sorians at least. He closed his eyes and focused; bright specs of aura invaded the darkness of his mind. He wrenched his eyes open in surprise. Their aura levels had risen significantly since the last time he'd glimpsed them. How was this possible? He could feel their power growing before him. A pressure that was enclosing him from all angles. It was nothing like the auric pressure of their old man. It was cold and ruthless.

"So, this is the tournament," said Caim, appearing at his side. "I'm so excited I could die!"

Storm took a deep breath and nodded. His brother was right. This is what they lived for. All their training would soon be put to the test. Despite his eagerness, he couldn't help but feel little pangs of anxiety biting away at him. They came upon the crowd and settled near the back.

Storm's wandering eyes jumped from fighter to fighter. Most of them were considerably bigger than him and Caim, who looked like they might actually have been the smallest ones there, and the youngest no doubt. On the back of a fighter right before him was an enormous blade; his thoughts flickered back to when their old man had released Caim's Fallblade to its ultimate form. He looked at Caim.

"Did you ever figure out how to transform your blade?"

"Nope," said Caim. "I've tried a few times since then and it still won't work."

Storm turned back to the crowd of fighters. They all wore such perfect armor; most with long white or black cloaks that fell gracefully down their backs. Several archers stood off in the shadows, their long wooden bows hung over their shoulders; some of them were sharpening green-tipped arrows with whetstones. Warriors with long spears, axes, and hammers all stood around idly. As his eyes tried to take everything in, he felt as if he were spinning around the crowd. He could feel it; these Sorians were no ordinary fighters. Each was battle-worn, keen, and no doubt either Colossus Hunters, Bounty Hunters, Mercenaries, or high ranking Nobility. Their bodies were haled and hard, and many had scars on their bodies or even their faces. Even the women were daunting to look at. Some were quite attractive, but with a deep power within. Storm could feel their auric pressure just from looking at their eyes.

"This is so exciting!" said Caim in glee.

Just then a massive man wearing only silver bracers and greaves turned around to face him. His chest was huge and bare; around his waist he wore a long sash that reached down to his knees. "Damn right there are. And you're looking at the strongest of them all right now!" He laughed a booming laugh and looked Caim dead in the eyes. "You're a pint-sized one aren't you, runt? And strange-lookin' in that armor to boot!"

But Caim wasn't even listening. He was staring straight past him at the fighter with the giant sword on his back. "That is so cool!" he said, poking Storm. If Storm didn't know any better he could have sworn one of the veins on the angered man's forehead ruptured.

Storm took a second to take in the sight of the massive man angered by Caim; a shield was fastened to his back and from his hands was a dangling chain that attached to a huge iron ball cracking the stone at his feet. A few feet to their side a silver-haired swordsman glanced over at Storm. He watched

Storm smirk at the towering man and sighed.

Far ahead in the crowd, past where Storm could see, an old man with long scarlet robes and golden stitching walked past the crowd and up onto a podium. A loud roar erupted from the crowd as he turned to face them. For a few long seconds, he took in all the eyes of the crowd, weighing them. And then he spoke.

"Welcome, brave warriors, to the 250th Soldier Games!!"

Storm moved to the side until he could see the old man clearly. He had long, pure white hair and an even longer white beard; one so great in length that it made Ronin's look short. His voice was loud and deep and he spoke with resolution and clarity, as if he had done this every cycle since the very first games. He wore slim spectacles, and it seemed to Storm that as he stared through them, he was surveying in more ways than one the potential winners of the games. It was then that Storm caught the old man's eyes and the old man his; for a flicker of an instant it was as if everyone had vanished and it was only Storm and the old man remaining in a shrouded realm. He felt an olden presence leaking forth and tried to look away but couldn't. He suddenly felt within the old man's eyes the same feeling as staring at an old tree, timeless and ancient and gleaming with mystery. A strange grin curved on the old man's lips and just like that, the trance was broken.

"Now, now," he spoke deeply, trying to calm the shouting and cheering. "I see some familiar faces and some new ones." He glanced to a lone swordsman wearing all white with a blood red bracers; jagged crimson hair fell just above his sky blue eyes. His skin was as dark as charcoal, with the slightest hints of red. On his back was a sword of the like Storm had never seen before. The blade was crystal blue with an ancient language carved into the edge; the hilt was layered with pale skulls, darkened by dirt that had never been cleaned, and the handle was wrapped in blood-stained ribbon that waved from the end in the light wind.

The old man's eyes were locked on the swordsman in white, "It's good to see you return, Squall Risier. Many believed you had it won last games. I am glad to see you look as strong as ever."

Storm watched the lone swordsman, whom he noticed no one stood within fifteen feet of, bow his eyes with only the slightest movement.

He's strong, thought Storm. *He's the strongest swordsman here by a longshot. And there is something strange about that sword … I get an eerie vibe from it, like I've seen a ghost. Bizarre.*

Storm turned his eyes to the distant sky. He couldn't help but feel as if it were some kind of miracle that had allowed them to get this far. He didn't believe in fate, but this was one of those moments that he doubted his belief, if only momentarily.

"To all of you who are here again, and to those of you who have come to test your strength anew, may the light of Vale shine upon your souls and guide your blades to victory!" Another eruption of cheering rose from the crowd.

Caim turned to Storm. "This is going to be so awesome! How entire childhood we spent training, and even though we always just did it for fun, this will be the truest way to test our strengths!"

Storm wanted to tell him to stop shouting and drawing attention, but he didn't. He felt the same excitement as Caim. They had never experienced anything like this growing up in Neverend, and they were definitely going to seize the opportunity to challenge their own limits.

A few feet to their side and unbeknownst to them stood a young boy their age with golden hair. On the edge of his left forearm was a round buckler, and on the other forearm, a miniature crossbow folded together. He wore a tight blue jacket, unzipped with the sleeves rolled up; a curved silver blade hung down from the back of his waist.

The old man on the podium coughed slightly. "For any of you who don't know—though it's certainly doubtful—I am Grandmaster Arius, one of the Strategic Elders to the Empress. Immediately, everyone in the crowd threw their elbows out, giving the sorian salute of Nobility. Everyone that is, except for Caim and Storm, who stood with their arms crossed. Storm felt Arius' intrigued glance fall on his once again and a nervous angst was roused in his soul.

The gold haired stranger watched curiously as the black-haired boy elbowed the silver-haired boy next to him who laughed, and then both of them gave the salute a few seconds too late. The silver-haired boy, who was wearing sandals gave a salute that was completely wrong.

"Fighters these days," the boy muttered. *These two clearly have no idea what they are fighting for. The Soldier Games isn't a joke that you enter to try and get some girlfriend. Hopefully they don't get killed off in the first ten minutes.* He flicked his gold hair from his blue eyes and gazed back up at the podium. *I've come too far to worry about others,* he thought.

Grandmaster Arius spoke again. "I assume all of you who have come understand the risk you take in entering." Storm felt Arius's presence once again upon him and did not meet his gaze. Arius continued, "In the past twenty cycles, there has unfortunately been no winner of the Soldier Games, though the prowess of Squall Rasier last games was certainly close. There are no guarantees that any of you will survive, although it has been quite a long time since we had a *Black Games* and normally, there are at least a few who make it through. However, know that all possible measures are taken regarding your safety. Nevertheless, there are still casualties—significant casualties—each time the Games occur."

"What's a Black Games?" whispered a young girl in a shaky voice.

"It's what they call the tournament if every contestant dies," answered an older warrior in a gruff voice. The girl's eyes grew wide as full moons.

Storm felt the ambiance of the crowd shift. Those who had looked so confident no longer seemed so powerful. It was as if Arius's words brought on a cloud of darkness that slithered into the hearts of all the fighters. The old man wasn't lying. The Games were not a joke, and he could feel it.

"We do what we can to prevent deaths ... but the ferocity of the trials make that difficult for us. There are some *things* ... out of our control. That is why, every cycle, I ask those of you who have come, to evaluate within yourself why it is that you are here. This is not the time to try to impress anyone. This is not the place to win honor. This is not a tournament for the faint of heart. This is a trial for those who are willing place their lives on the line to achieve victory. *Therefore*, if any of you harbor any doubts, I ask that you look deeply within yourself and ask this question: Are you here for the right reasons? Do not let the rumors sway your minds. This tournament *will* kill you if you are unprepared ... and I hate to see the blood of good sorians lost when perhaps what you need is simply more time, more experience ... or stronger purpose."

The crowd of fighters grew fidgety. Storm looked up as several of the contestants started backing away. Not once did they turn their back to Grandmaster Arius, but left with a subtle nod, so subtle that Storm could barely perceive it. The contestants found their way out of the crowd. Storm caught the face of one man, large and powerful looking, but his face was paler than a cold moon, and a thick sweat was dripping from his brow. Storm swallowed hard. He could feel the man's fear; almost as if the man himself were not before Storm, but his fear, a shadow of his doubts running away, consuming all that once was confident.

After several of the contestants had left, Grandmaster Arius raised an eyebrow. "Now then, I can feel that those of you who have stayed have found your resolve. I would not be able to live with myself were I to send those into the games who would not have made it. Those who have stayed, your eyes have met mine. You are ready. You have come because of the causes you believe in, or perhaps for the realization of a cause greater than yourself." Storm felt the intensity of the auras grow heavier. The pressure of their energy pushed down on him. The ones that stayed were determined. He could feel it. He made a fist, cracking his knuckles.

"As all of you know, the Soldier Games is a compilation of three trials. I am here to announce the three trials chosen for this cycle's games by the Weavelocks of Fate."

Storm looked at Caim and raised an eyebrow. For all

he knew, the tournament was just about fighting strong opponents.

"Now then, the first trial this cycle and a personal favorite of mine will be, the *Chasing of the Scarves!*"

Storm noticed that several of the smaller contestants were grinning, while the larger contestants became solemn. He wondered if it was a contest of speed, rather than power.

Caim nudged Storm, "Na neo, what's the Chasing of the Scarves?"

Storm turned very slowly to face his brother. "You know, last cycle when I did this it involved chasing scarves attached to sky monkeys in a circle …"

Caim's eyes narrowed, "You did this last cycle without me!?"

Storm barely clasped his hand over his brother's mouth, but not before a few sorians turned their eyes toward the two. A couple of the fighters stared back at them strangely. The boy with the blond hair stood behind them, staring oddly at the two brothers. He muttered under his breath, *"Something's off with these two …"*

"You got a problem?" said Storm, staring back at the couple sorians. After a second they turned back to the podium. The silver haired swordsman that had been staring at Storm earlier met his eyes and smirked, "Maybe I do, maybe I don't. I guess you'll have to wait till the games begin to find out." He turned his back to Storm who clenched his fist but didn't speak.

"You idiot!" Storm whispered harshly to Caim. "How am I supposed to know what it is? I never did this either, you know!"

"I didn't think you would lie to me …" said Caim, quietly.

Storm felt as though he'd been struck. "I wasn't lying, Caim … stop being stupid. I was kidding."

"As I'm sure you all know," said Grandmaster Arius, "only the first 18 of you to catch your scarves will be admitted to the second trial. And it looks like …" He surveyed the crowd. "There's still well over a hundred of you remaining. It seems as though this cycle is going to be a rough."

Storm couldn't believe it. There were easily a hundred sorians yet only 18 would pass the first trial? And if this wasn't a trial of fighting … then what was it?

"The finalists from the first trial will be paired into teams of three, then following a brief break when the residents of Risia and Falia enter the Arena of Kings, the second trial will begin. The second trial of this cycle's games will be, the *Ascendance of Falling Tower*. Much unlike the Chasing of the Scarves, the Ascendance of Falling Tower is more of a mental challenge. All great warriors understand that having great strength alone is not enough. The tower challenges all that lies within… ."

The crowd grew deadly silent at the announcement of the second challenge. One of the remaining contestants fell to his knees, his eyes sinking to the stone.

"Out of all the trials that can be played …" he whispered, "We have the luck of the cursed. The Weavelocks of Fate haven't chosen Falling Tower in over 100 cycles."

Dark thoughts swam through Storm's mind as he tried to figure out what awaited them in the mysterious tower. Whatever it was, Arius seemed to want to discourage them before they had even begun. The Grandmaster's words seemed an ill omen.

"And the last trial …" said Arius grimly, "is …" Everyone's ears perked up. Arius met their stern gazes with a look of silence, and then cracked a smile and laughed. "Ho-ho-ho, it seems I have forgotten!"

Storm raised a weary eyebrow. Caim started laughing. The contestants stood in mouth wide awe.

"Ah!" cried Arius, snapping his fingers. "I have caught it!" He made a motion like he was catching a fly out of the air. "My memory that is!"

Caim leaned over to Storm, "I like this old man. I bet him and grandpa would be friends."

Storm nodded, "You would think that. Now let's see what this final trial is gonna be."

Arius took a deep breath and his grin faded as he spoke. "The final trial this cycle will be the original finale of the Games. It is the *Raising of the Flags* to be held in the fabled Arena of Kings! Although you must note that in this cycle there have been several changes. The last trial will be one in which your resolves will be put to the ultimate test. You will see what awaits you in the Arena of Kings. That is, *if* you can make it that far. All I can promise you is that it will be the greatest challenge you have ever faced in your entire lives. If you wish to taunt Death, if you wish to test your abilities to the highest degree of challenge, you have come to the place of unforgiving."

His eyes scanned the crowd, seeking any who might have lost their resolve. He continued, "But should you succeed, you will enter into a life you cannot imagine. You will dedicate your life to protecting that which we hold most dearly. The lives of those we cherish, from the very thing which threatens all. We maintain the balance of all things within the Great Void. Never forget that. Our people, we are the unseen heroes that sacrifice everything to keep all life safe. Death's gaze misses nothing. This tournament, this trial … it separates the real from the myth and legend." Around them, the statues of previous victors seemed to glimmer with pride. They stood before the contestants as legends.

"Well then!" Arius said. "It seems those who have lost the willpower to fight have fled. I applaud those who have remained. But your fight is not over, it has only just begun."

Storm felt his heart starting to race. He had not imagined that he would feel so threatened before even starting the tournament. His heartbeat had sped considerably.

"We will now begin the Opening Ceremonies and the preparations for the Catching of the Scarves," said Arius. "For those of you who would like to watch, young Master Atreyu here will be forming Aura Bubbles, or *Airvras*, so you may watch the preparation of the course and also, might I add, the opening speech from the Divine Empress of Soria, Lady Aurora Ne'Fair!"

The Empress is going to be here!? Storm had heard stories of the Empress and wondered what her speech would entail, or if he would even get to see her.

"Storm!" cried Caim, "we're going to see the Empress!"

Storm grabbed Caim's shoulder, "Caim, I swear to the gods, if you keep screaming I'll kill you myself …"

Caim lifted his head trying to see through the crowd. At the base of the podium was a young Sorian sitting with his legs crossed; he wore similar scarlet robes to Arius but his hair was completely shaven. Storm stood on his tiptoes to try and get a better view as Atreyu held his palms up in front of him; several misty bubbles of aura were born from his fingertips before growing rapidly in size and moving out amongst the crowd for everyone to see. The last bubble of aura lingered directly before Master Atreyu.

"What is that?" asked Caim. Storm didn't answer.

"And with that I leave you be, to mingle amongst yourselves, and to prepare yourselves … for this cycle's Soldier Games!" Several of the contestants roared fiercely while others merely averted their eyes and nodded.

Storm took a deep breath. This was it. Soon they would be competing in the greatest tournament of the worlds. There was no turning back now, not that he would have even if given the chance. He looked around. It seemed like anyone who thought Caim and Storm didn't belong had completely forgotten about them. They blended in amongst a sea of armor.

I wonder what kind of tests these three trials are, thought Storm.

"Alright Caim, let's just lay low until the games start." He turned to find that Caim had disappeared. "Great," he said under his breath. "Just great." Just as he was leaving to look for Caim he came face to face with the same gold haired stranger who had been eyeing them earlier.

"Oi there," said the boy with seeking eyes. Storm immediately noticed a strange accent. He eyed Storm's strange armor, then waved his hand in the arc of a setting sun. "I'm

Ladon, an engineer of sorts and inventor."

Storm wasn't sure whether to use his real name or not at this point. He shrugged thoughts of the future off, realizing that they would probably be caught sooner or later. "Storm," he said repeating the same action, and braced himself for the boy's response.

"Storm, huh? Haven't heard of you before, which branch are you with?"

Storm felt his stomach turn; maybe getting caught was going to be sooner rather than later. Quickly, he tried to think of something he could say, but before he could say a word, Ladon spoke again.

"I get it," he said. "You're nervous, huh? I don't blame you mate, this is my first time, too."

Storm felt like he couldn't have been any luckier and quickly responded, "I don't know about nervous, but I'm definitely something."

Ladon forced a laugh. "Yeah … that speech was, well, not really helpful for those who have already vowed to go through with this."

Storm felt a flicker of irritation as the noble boy continued talking to him—he needed to go find Caim. But he also had to avoid doing anything another noble wouldn't do. The problem was, he had no idea what another noble would do.

Ladon suddenly looked past Storm; something had caught his attention. Storm turned slowly, hoping, praying, that it wasn't Caim. Yet, there was Caim, standing at the front of the crowd an inch away from one of the airvras and staring at it from every direction. He could hear his brother from where he stood.

"This is so *cool*!" Caim quickly sidestepped around the massive airvras. "You have to teach me how to do this!"

Ladon grinned. "Your mate is … not so nervous I guess."

"Being a moron will do that to you."

Ladon laughed, "Moron or not, I wish I had his enthusiasm. He doesn't seem fazed at all about the games. You know, I ran the mathematics for the probability of survival using data from the past 249 Games. We have more than a 51 percent chance of Death here." He shivered. "There have been 36,391 competitors before us over the cycles. Of those, 19,201 have died in the Games. It's pretty crazy how close this is to a suicide wish. And that's not even the worst part ... you ready? There have only been 74 winners, *ever*." He paused, watching Caim's ridiculous antics. "But for some reason, just watching your mate makes me feel more at ease. It's like he doesn't even realize there's mathematically a stupidly high chance of dying in this tournament. C'mon, let's go see what he's up to. I want to figure out where he gets his courage from."

"Great ... just great," said Storm before following Ladon through the crowd.

"Whoa ..." said Caim, staring in the airvras. "I can see all of Soria through this thing. How are you doing this!?" Caim watched as many sorians from the western and eastern wings gathered to the edge of their lands. Some brought picnic baskets and blankets, others were climbing trees to get a better view. The more he watched the more he realized that thousands and thousands of sorians were gathering to watch the Soldier Games. The entirety of both worlds would be watching.

A sudden voice broke Caim's focus. "Never seen one of these before?" asked Ladon.

Caim didn't even look up. "Nope, never. This is seriously so cool. How does this work?"

Ladon raised an eyebrow. "Could've sworn this was something everyone knew about." He stared at Caim's armor realizing that it didn't fit well. Glancing back to Storm, he found that the bulbous armor didn't seem appropriate for Storm's physique either.

"Oi, bubble boy," said Caim, bonking Atreyu on the head. "Aren't you going to answer me?"

Ladon's expression froze, and he quickly grabbed Caim's hand and pulled him back. "Whoa there, mate! You can't interfere with the Projectors! That's a serious crime!"

Storm walked up just in time to catch the end of Ladon's sentence. "Projectors?"

Master Atreyu hadn't even budged from his position, but something about the way Atreyu's face twitched made all three of them feel a bit uncomfortable. Ladon looked at Storm even more strangely. "Yeah … Projectors, you know, the ones who project the games across all of Soria for everyone to see?"

Ladon turned to Caim. "Just don't touch them, they'll kick you out of the games."

Caim looked up at Ladon, and then turned to Storm. "Who's this guy?"

Ladon looked taken back. "Um uhh … Ladon. And you?"

Caim turned to face Ladon very slowly. Storm felt his instincts alerting him to something. He noticed something off about his brother's expression, and then it struck him. The expression on Caim's face was very close to thoughtfulness. A dark foreboding was forming in Storm's mind when Caim finally spoke.

"I'm Geoerge. Nice to meet you, Laboon."

Storm nearly smacked his own forehead. He could tell Caim was immensely proud of himself. And for *Geoerge*? *That wasn't even a name!* He wanted to punch Caim. Strangle him. Kick him and throw him off the bridge.

Ladon looked at him very carefully. "You're name is Geoerge? Never heard of a name like that before. Not that I mean that in a negative way. And by the way it's *Ladon*, not Laboon."

Storm felt like their situation was growing more precarious by the second. Not only had Caim thought up a name that no one had ever even heard before, it was completely and utterly random, as if he just pieced together arbitrary syllables.

"Yep, Geoerge," said Caim proudly.

"Uh, well, it's a pleasure," said Ladon.

Storm immediately tried to change the subject and without thinking, pointed at the airvras.

"Hey, what's this?"

The airvras was about the size of Storm's torso and flowed

with a bluish energy that reminded him of clear running water. He reached out, touching it, and the aura seemed to grab to his fingers, stretching out from the bubble slightly before sucking back to it. It was an eerie feeling, and the opening of Atreyu's eyes told him that he shouldn't do it again. Staring into it, he felt as if he were watching a world from outside a world, and he wondered briefly if Lady Vale watched them as he was watching others now, if she even existed.

He watched the airvras project images from all of Soria. Images of the white castle, Aurora's Light, soon came before his eyes. It was the most intricately built thing he had ever seen. Everything he had always imagined it to be, it was. It had in every aspect, the exact opposite feel to Falia. The great towers stretched up as if seeking the heavens. He realized that Aurora's Light was not just a castle, but that it was a great white city—the castle only lay in the center of it, surrounded by four tall towers. Outside the four towers were eight other towers rising from a circular wall that surrounded the city.

So this is the home of the nobles … No wonder they looked down on a city like Trestles. Storm didn't want to admit it, but Aurora's Light was astounding in comparison to Falia's capital. It truly shined.

After a second the airvras switched to images of Neverend and many of the villages on Falia including the capital of Trestles. It wasn't long before the scenery changed. Within the airvras, many other young boys with shaven heads were creating hundreds of airvras all around Soria.

"There's more of them …" said Storm, not realizing he was speaking out loud.

"Those are just the Projectors setting up the stage for the first trial," said Ladon. "Soon they should be—here they go." The three of them watched as the airvras focused on a very old man sitting on the edge of a cliff. A long silver cloak hung over his shoulders but beneath he wore nothing but torn pants; he looked of mostly skin and bone. His face was incredibly wrinkled and for a second, Storm thought he might be terribly sick. Sitting on the ground next to him was a strange-looking device; curvy and wide at the base, but as it reached up from the ground it grew quite slender. Near the rim was a flat circular piece of stone and above that was some type of brazier with flaming hot coals upon it. Stretching out and into the hand of the old man was a long blade of hollow wood.

"That is the strangest-looking thing ever ..." muttered Storm.

"A device for smoking, believe it or not," said Ladon. "But doing so takes a horrible toll on your body. You see his hair, thin and sparse and looking as if it's about to fall out? His hands and his face, wrinkled so? Some of the Committee of Health tried to ban the invention, but ultimately the fate of those lies in their own hands, or so was the final verdict."

Storm began to feel more and more aggravated about Ladon's presence. Why was he hanging around them? Didn't he have anyone else here he could be talking to? He wondered for a second if Ladon was suspicious about them. He turned back to the airvras and watched as the old man held up the blade of hollow wood to his mouth and took a deep breath. A few moments later he opened his mouth wide and his throat pulsed.

"What's he doing?" But Caim could barely finish his sentence before shouting, "Cool!"

Storm watched as the old man blew a ring of smoke that rose out before him, growing larger and larger until he could have thrown a house through it. It floated out over the edge of the cliff and into the sky until it came to a stop and didn't move, or fade. The airvras switched angles until the three of them could see several rings of smoke taking their places around Risia and Falia.

"Those rings are the checkpoints we pass through during the race," said Ladon. "They're called Enhancement Rings. That old man is an *Enhancer*. He has the ability to give any sorian all kinds of abilities, good or bad. The aura in his lungs weaves through the smoke and that's why they never fade. Not unless he wants them to, that is. See, if you look closely at the smoke, you can see the faint strings of black energy. During the Chasing of the Scarves, these rings are the checkpoints and upon flying through them, they gift your body with either a good or bad enhancement. It can be the difference between winning and losing in this race." Ladon paused. "Well, I guess it's not really a race. You just have to catch your scarf, really. Easier said than done though, that's for certain."

Storm tried to avert his mind from the part where Ladon said they would be flying. He tried to imagine a different type of trial, one other than them flying around the floating lands of Risia and Falia, flying through rings of smoke and trying to catch ... scarves. It still wasn't making sense.

"What kind of Enhancements?" Caim asked.

Ladon shook his head. "I honestly don't know, they change from cycle to cycle. You know, to keep things fresh for the audience, while keeping things difficult for the contestants."

Caim watched as Ladon reach beneath his jacket to pull out the winged key hanging around his neck. "When you fly through the ring, the enhancement enters your key and it begins to glow. Then you have the opportunity to either activate the enhancement or not, simply clicking the wings together like this." He folded the wings of the key together, which made a faint *clicking* sound. "Genius really ... I would have loved to see how they designed these. I've worked on similar things in my day, but nothing like the stuff they use for the games."

Storm reached down and grabbed his key. He hadn't realized how important it really was to the games. To his side, Caim peered closer and closer at the airvras. The view had changed and was now focused back on Aurora's Light.

"Storm, look! The castle! We've never seen it this close before!" Caim was in awe and made no effort to disguise it. Storm felt his apprehension gurgling up inside of him like lava in a volcano. Surely Ladon must have caught on to them by now.

"Yeah," said Ladon, "I don't get to see the castle much

from where I work. I got stationed at the furthest tip of Risia, not far from Starseeker, the Tower of the Damned. They don't let me go too close to the castle." He couldn't avert his eyes from the airvras. Storm could sense a slight change in his tone after mentioning the castle.

"What's Starseeker?" asked Caim, "Tower of the Damned?" Storm felt his heart skip a beat.

Ladon looked very strangely at Caim, "You're joking right?"

Storm put a strong arm around Caim's neck and laughed, "He's a bit of a joker, this one," laughed Storm, squeezing tightly. Caim's eyes swelled for a moment and Storm let go of him. He put his hand behind his head and smiled, "Sorry, I like to joke around. But hold on one second …" He grabbed Storm and pulled him a few feet away.

"I really wanna know what that is! Don't you!?" whispered Caim.

"Seriously Caim, I'm going to kill you. You *do* realize we're dead if we get caught right? Shut up and we'll figure out what the stupid Tower of the Damned is later!" He walked back to Ladon as Caim's eyes burnt holes into his back.

Storm came to a stop before Ladon, who luckily had gotten distracted by an argument between two contestants. He glanced at his brother. How much longer could this go on without them being given away? He hated how Caim didn't take anything seriously. He didn't think about consequences. He just wanted to have fun, and even if they got caught, he'd probably consider that an adventure too.

Ladon reached out and touched Storm's shoulder. Storm nearly jumped. "The games will start soon, so I hope you're ready. I hope I'm ready."

Storm felt a spike of anger as Ladon's noble hand touched him. He didn't know how or why, but for some reason just being touched by a noble irritated him. He wanted to break his fingers, but he held back. He wondered why he was feeling such anger recently. He felt something different within himself. He shook off the ominous feeling and looked back to the airvras. It was focused in on the central tower, the highest tower in all of Soria. The image of the castle spun around, gaining altitude little by little.

"Listen," said Ladon. "Our Empress is about to speak."

XLIII – Empress Aurora Ne'Fair

The White Castle known as Aurora's Light is one of beauty and brilliance. It was birthed from two of the greatest minds of all time: the architectural genius Alani Pooks, who designed the blueprint shortly after the crowning of the Empress, and the renowned philosopher and creator of Alchemy, Lord Galileo, who used his alchemic creations to bring to life the legendary castle and its city.

Two outer curtain walls make up the perimeter, crafted of the finest ore in all of Soria—Aurelian. The outermost wall is over a hundred feet thick and from it rise eight towers that guard the city night and day. Within the outer wall lies the sacred city, Lasilia. Next is the second curtain wall and from it rise the four great towers, the headquarters of the Force and the Shield—guardians of the castle and the Empress, which lay just within them. And rising from the center of the castle is the last and tallest tower, home to the Empress of Soria—the Spearway to Eden is its name. Some believe that only upon the tip of this tower does one have the chance of glimpsing

Vale's Garden; a nirvanic land shrouded in mist and legend, existing yet not existing.

Deep within the base of the Empress's tower lies a grand hall in the shape of an X, with each point connecting to one of the four great towers of the Force and Shield. The walls of the grand hall are lined with bright and colorful glass depicting ancient warriors and images of the beautiful lands of Risia and Falia (including the much renowned Skyfalls and the great trees Nocturnis Aqua and Aquas Eternis). The inside of the grand hall is something to be mesmerized by, for painted along its ceiling is a legendary mural depicting the ancient war of Eiendrahk—the War of Gods. Painted by one of the Firstborn, the Virtuoso Jiselangelo, the work of art is an uncontested masterpiece, and elicits awe from whoever lays eyes upon it. It has been said that if you focus your eyes in just the right manner, the painting comes to life before you, telling a story of old. However, as you remove your gaze from the painting, so is the story removed from your memory, allowing you to relive the story for the first time, every time.

It is within this grand hall, that on the day of these particular Soldier Games, a gathering had been called—a gathering of the four most powerful soldiers of the Two Worlds.

- - - -

Lady Scylla's silver heels echoed as she made her way into the hall. Laid over her traditional royal armor were ceremonial feathers and thin garments of white silk that hung over her body with all the grace of a queen. Peering out through her emerald eye, she found Lady Sakura standing still in the center of the hall. Draped over her shoulders was her long white vice captain's jacket and an ornate long bow; a dark leather quiver of arrows hung from her hip.

In the far corner Sakura noticed another dark figure: Vice Captain Vasuki, who was leaning against a wall with his eyes closed. Beneath his hooded black cloak one could see the bandages wrapping his frail ribs, and the gold bracelets circling his forearms. He stood with his usual uncaring demeanor, his black hair hanging to the right side of his pale and sunken face. Upon hearing her Captain's footsteps, Sakura turned and kneeled.

"Welcome, my Captain."

Vasuki opened one of his eyes and watched Lady Scylla approach the center of the room. Her eye caught his. He couldn't help but feel a chill shiver up his spine. Not only was she considered the most powerful Sorian, she was perhaps the strongest advocate of justice and the upholding of the Great Laws. How many seconds could he last in a fight with her? All he would have to do was take her other eye, a task that seemed as challenging as taming the light of the sun. He frowned, knowing full well that even without her sight, she would certainly destroy him in a fight.

A door banged shut at the end of the farthest hall, and Lord Falkor trudged towards them. His golden armor was radiant as usual and he wore upon his back his grand and majestic shield, all white and lined with gems of many colors. Vasuki raised an eyebrow as he gazed upon the silver and scarlet cloak wrapped around his Captain's neck, which was flowing down behind him as he walked.

Sakura raised her arm in the Sorian salute as she bowed her head. "Lord Falkor, it is an undying honor."

"Bwahaha!" Lord Falkor bellowed, his voice echoing many times through the grand hall. "Yeh as well meh dear! Congratulations on yeh ascension to Vice Captain. Da first in all'a history teh do what yeh did. Yeh have quite da soldier here, Miss Scylla." He turned his gaze to Lady Scylla who was staring at him through sharpened eyes.

"You're late," she said.

Lord Falkor smiled heartily. "Miss Scylla, nice teh see yeh as well." He looked around. "Can't help but get a bit excited when all four'a us are in da same room togetha!"

Vasuki closed his eyes and didn't move from his position against the wall.

"Vasuki, yeh came!" Lord Falkor shouted. "Had meh

worried there fer a moment!"

"Seems you've still yet to discipline your rebellious vice-captain," Lady Scylla said, staring at Vasuki. "He should learn some respect. Such a disgrace before the Empress is—"

"No disrespect to yerself Miss Scylla," Lord Falkor said, "but I believe that matters of the Shield might just be outta yer jurisdiction."

Before Lady Scylla could answer, Lord Falkor began laughing again. "Bwahaha, les not be fightin amongst ourselves jus yet! Today is a day to watch da fightin of da up and comin!" His gaze suddenly became serious. "And we need teh be on our toes …"

Vasuki grinned under his hood, sincerely hoping that those of the Rogue X were stupid enough to try playing with fire. He had been aching to stretch his muscles for quite some time now.

"I take it you have organized the guarding of the inner and outer perimeters?" asked Lady Scylla.

Lord Falkor nodded. "It has been done. Nothin be gettin past those walls today. I trust yeh have taken care'a yer end?"

"Your trust is well placed."

Their conversation was interrupted as a robed and hooded man scurried his way into the center of the hall. He came within ten paces of Lady Scylla and lowered himself to his knee, bowing to her. "I apologize for my intrusion, Captains and Vice Captains of the noble Force and Shield. The Divine Empress is prepared to see you now." Lady Scylla raised her hand just slightly and the hooded man rose to his feet and backed out of the room, never once turning his back to them.

Lord Falkor turned and looked at Vasuki. "Alright then, les go."

With difficulty Vasuki stood up straight. He took hold of his massive hammer and started creeping towards the center of the room, dragging the enormous thing behind him on the floor the whole way by its sleek, long black handle.

Sakura raised an eyebrow; for a Vice Captain he looked exceptionally weak. He even had to reach back once or twice with both hands to pull the weapon over little cracks in the stone floor. Sakura bit her lip in an attempt to stifle a laugh. She had heard that Vasuki's strength was on par with Lord Falkor's, although she never had the opportunity of seeing him fight. She'd only conversed with him several times, and each conversation had birthed bad impressions. The only surefire things she knew about Lord Vasuki were that he was impatient, had an intense bloodlust, and lived with the sole goal of killing his own Captain in order to take his place. A horrible candidate for a Vice Captain, or so she thought.

Lady Scylla watched impatiently as he dragged his hammer. "You have quite the nerve to take any chance of tarnishing the stone of this hall."

Vasuki took his place next to Lord Falkor. "Guess I'm lucky this stone is made of Aurelian and can't be scratched no matter how hard I try."

"Yeah, lucky I'm in a good mood today," replied Lady Scylla. She stared at him grimly. "You should thank your fate every single day that you were born a man and not a woman. Not like you would have what it takes to be one of the Force were you a woman anyway."

"Trust me, I don't," muttered Vasuki. Scylla shot him a dark look, but Falkor held out his arm between the two. "It's time ta meet da Empress. Let's get goin." He turned and held his palm face down over the ground.

A circular black ring appeared around the four of them on the stone, and a black podium rose from the center. Lord Falkor reached out and placed his enormous fingertips on five tiny white gems. When he lifted his hand they began to glow.

"*Ascend*," he said in a deep voice. The floor began to tremble as the ring darkened and a circular platform lifted them up and rose up to the ceiling. Just as Vasuki thought they'd be crushed against the enormous mural of the Sun, a point of light appeared in its center and grew larger and larger as a hidden door twisted open. As soon as they passed through the ceiling, the velocity of their ascent increased tenfold.

Vasuki turned to look at Sakura as they were rising.

"Can't say I'm not surprised to see you here …" He sneered evilly. "After all, it must have been some sort of trick?"

"Vasuki," she replied with a glare. "Can't say I'm not surprised you're able to hold yourself upright after exhausting yourself by simply walking across the room." Vasuki's eyes turned to rage but he did not speak. Sakura turned her gaze away as they climbed steadily, and then she felt it—a cold hand on her shoulder and a dark whisper in her ear.

"You'll see what I am capable of soon enough."

She turned back but Vasuki wasn't anywhere near her. He was standing behind Lord Falkor with his arms crossed and eyes closed. Had she imagined it? No, definitely not. He had just been there, and it was his voice that had spoken. But how? There was something ominous about him. The way his mind worked was … different, as if he were perpetually planning something no other could guess.

It wasn't long before the platform sealed itself in place on the highest floor. The four of them gazed around the much smaller chamber that they had just entered. Upon the walls were several paintings depicting warm colors and vivid scenery. The ceiling was painted black, pricked with hundreds of celestial fires that created the feeling of a most memorable starry night. On both sides of the room kneeled a dozen soldiers in all black armor, each of which were adorned with red ribbons around their left arms. A single dark door lay hidden within the wall behind the soldiers on the right side of the room. Their heads bowed low, averting their eyes for the arrival of the Captains. Long banners depicting the symbols of the Force, three spears rising from a crimson sun, and the Shield, a blue-eyed dragon curving around a beautiful woman, fell from the walls around them. At the far end of the room was a scarlet carpet leading up seven stairs to a large ornate chair; just beyond it was a final banner—the sigil of the Empress. Sitting in the chair was none other than the Empress herself.

The four of them walked forward three steps then took a knee and bowed their heads. The soldiers along the walls all touched their foreheads to the ground. The Empress regarded them silently for a moment and then stood. The four of them lifted their heads. She was as beautiful as a shooting star before a midnight sky. Proud and benevolent she was, and each of the soldiers who stole a glance of her were breath-taken. A brilliant crimson dress flowed over the perfection of her body, and cutouts revealed the fairness of her skin just below her breasts. Her hair fell like long strands of white sunlight all the way to her naked feet. Twined into the tresses of her white locks was a black dragon-wing diadem, glittering with several deep-set rubies.

She gazed at them through deep emerald eyes, smiling in such a manner that all who looked upon her felt that they were in the presence of an ethereal being. A calming energy permeated the room, and the tension ceased to exist. Falling from her neck was the crystal pendent Lorienia, whose perfection could never be equaled by another gem. The beauty of the gem—and its wearer—could not be captured in words, or songs, or paintings. Only in the moment could the beauty of Lorienia be seen and understood, and after, its comprehension vanished to once again be misunderstood, much like the beauty of the Empress herself.

She walked gracefully down the stairs, her naked feet making no sound. Upon stepping down off the last stair, all of the soldiers in the in the room pushed their foreheads harder into the stone. And just at that moment there was a startling *crash* as the Empress tripped over her dress and tumbled to the ground. The nearest soldiers were on their feet in an instant to help, but the Empress waved them away and jumped to her feet a little too quickly.

"We're alright! We're ok!" she said, laughing under her breath. "Gosh, we're so nervous!" She looked at the Captains, who all continued to kneel with their mouths open, shocked. She straightened her dress and her hair, and blushed deeply.

Soldiers turned to look at each other in complete and utter shock. Vasuki didn't know what to think. The room fell silent, at a loss for how to react appropriately. Sakura watched

XLIII – EMPRESS AURORA NE'FAIR

as the Empress collected herself and then pretended it never happened, although her face continued to flush red. She walked before them and before the Captains could speak, she spoke, her soft red lips almost singing to them.

"Please, raise your heads and stand," she began. "We can't help but feel a little uneasy before the heroes of Soria, who bow their heads so graciously towards us." Vasuki's ears twitched for a moment at the use of the word *us*. The Empress was considered to be the heart of Soria and thus spoke as if she was a piece of the land itself, as if her heart and the heart of Soria were one and the same. Hearing her speak was something that took some getting used too.

Lord Falkor was the first to recover. He beamed. "Yeh are lookin as beautiful as eveh my lady."

Lady Scylla's eyes flared towards him angrily. "Such blatant disrespect should not be tolerated. Address the Empress with the respect she deserves, and use the proper tongue."

"It's quite alright, Lady Scylla," said the Empress. "We must understand how different we can be from one another and accept those with differences for who they are, as sorians."

Lady Scylla bowed her head, "My apologies."

The Empress smiled and looked towards the ceiling. "Speaking of our sorians, we mustn't keep them waiting." She walked forward and stood next to the two Captains. "Shall we?"

"Yes, my lady," the four of them spoke in unison. Kneeling at the Empress's side, Lady Scylla spoke the word "Ascend," and the circular platform once again rose up, passing through a new twisting hole in the ceiling.

The speed of the platform quickened. Vasuki could smell the fragrance of freshly blossomed flowers coming from the Empress and it made his nose twitch with interest. He much preferred the smell of blood, but for some odd reason, her fragrance was ecstatic to him. He shook his head violently. He needed to get away from her before he went crazy.

Sakura looked at Vasuki as he kept turning his head away and covering his nose. Strangely, he kept turning back and smelling before turning away again. She couldn't help but laugh under her breath at his antics. She looked over to the Empress who still seemed embarrassed about tripping on the staircase. It was an unbelievable feeling. Escorting the Empress to the Soldier Games. An incredible thing was happening, one of the highest honors any sorian could hold. She for a moment wished the ring lift ride would never end. In fact, it did seem as if they would just keep climbing indefinitely, but at last they passed through a final hole and into the light of Day. They were now standing atop the Spearway to Eden, one of the highest points in all of Soria. The only peak that rivaled its height was that of the Damned Tower, Starseeker, which bared its jagged tooth far away on the western edge of Risia.

The Empress took a deep breath and walked off the platform, stretching her arms up to the sky above her. "Feels … so … good," she said, yawning. The sky above was bright and warm and the sun had found her place in the center of it all.

In the far distance black clouds sat upon the horizon, and Sakura wondered if they were fleeing before the beauty of Aurora Ne'Fair. She had seen the Empress a few times before, but never spent more than a moment around her. She had to admit, she wasn't what she expected. Maybe someone more formal? More stern? The Empress reminded her of a young girl who was simply in love with the wonders of the world. Someone who didn't care for the politics or the pressing matters to which others became so attached.

The Empress came to a stop at a set of stairs that stretched up, arcing off the top of the tower.

"The Soldier Games are wonderful and sad at the same time," she said. "So many lives risked, so many lives lost. The courage of fighting for something greater than yourself … It's something we will never understand."

Lady Scylla spoke, "I believe you may understand best of all, my Empress."

Aurora bowed her eyes to Lady Scylla's kind words. Two Captains walked before her, flanked to her sides a single step in front. The Vice Captains followed and stood two paces behind, flanking their two captains.

"Alright then," said the Empress. "Let's go … and

let's hope we don't fall this time!" She cracked a smile and laughed at herself. "All these ages and I'm still as clumsy as ever."

Lady Scylla sighed with a smile on her face. Lord Falkor laughed heartily. Vasuki turned his nose away and Sakura wondered in gleeful awe.

XLIV – The Girl and the Nowl

ack in the land of Falia, far beyond Trestles and beyond the silver string of river that wound its way towards the Great Tree, walked a girl with a blue scarf staring out over the vast blue sky. Clouds hovered here and there, and she could taste the air; fresh and cool, as it always tasted just before a storm. She pulled behind her a giant cart of savory meats that *clanked* and *bumped* along the rough dirt path. She soon noticed a giant ring of smoke in the sky. After nearly an entire day of traveling, she had finally reached her destination.

Kodi reached up and pulled her blue scarf from around her neck, allowing her short jagged hair to fall free. No older than 11 cycles, childish features still showed strongly on her determined face. Dropping the handle of the cart, she turned to find one of the thousand airvras floating around both Risia and Falia.

The Games would begin soon. She could feel her heart racing. She had never attempted anything like what she was about to. The anticipation, if that's what it was, was killing her. It wouldn't be long before the Empress gave her opening speech to the world and kick–started the Games. She brought herself as close to the edge of the cliff as possible, staring intensely into the sky and searching for something in the distance.

XLIV – THE GIRL AND THE NOWL

Raising her fingers to her lips she whistled, loud and clear, and walked back to the cart, where she unstrapped the meat. A sudden flutter of wings alerted her to his arrival.

"Noctis!" she turned, smiling.

Behind her the massive jet black nowl landed; a species of bird known as the grandfather of owls, for they were nearly five to ten times larger than their distant cousins, and much smarter. They were extremely rare and renowned as one of the most intelligent creatures in all of Soria. For many cycles, nowls were believed to be celestial creatures, for they came from the god realm, Vale's Garden.

Noctis stood on his feet, which barely stuck out before his powerful feathered body. He stood nearly three times larger than Kodi and stared down at her through bright orange eyes, which flickered toward the wafting aromas coming from the cart. She couldn't help but grin as he waddled up to her, briefly taking a moment to lower his head and meet her tiny hand.

"Wow, you've gotten so big," she whispered. She watched as he walked up to the cart and tore into the first piece of meat. She approached him and ran her fingers down his soft yet muscular wing. Almost immediately he stopped eating and turned his massive eyes towards her and snapped his pointed beak.

"Oh, sorry!" she said. "Forgot you don't like to be touched while you're eating." She laughed a little, and she smiled, remembering the first time she'd figured that out... .

–   –   –   –

Kodi had grown up in a small cabin just north of Trestles. She was a vibrant young girl and extremely clever for her age. She spent most of her days exploring anything and everything. As she got older, she soon realized that the most adventurous areas to discover awaited her in Neverend.

She was raised by her grandfather who had woken up one morning to find her as a baby crying on the porch of his wooden house. She had never found out how she had come to be on his doorstep, and no clues existed to bring her closer to the truth. As she grew older she took an interest in the strange activities that captivated her grandfather from dusk till dawn. He was constantly fiddling with strange gems and all different kinds of things that intrigued her beyond belief.

"Grandpa, what are you doing?" she constantly pestered. He always had the same answer: "Alchemy my dear, Alchemy." To which she would always reply, "But grandpa, what's Alchemy?" She never forgot his wry smile upon her familiar question.

"Alchemy is the tool which will save all of Soria." His answer never changed, and from that day on, Kodi considered her grandpa as a hero to all of Soria, but especially to herself. She spent much time learning all she could about Alchemy in her spare time, and it soon became her favorite hobby. She learned quickly how to draw transmutation circles, and what was needed for the aid in deconstructing and rebuilding. The rules of Alchemy became engraved in her mind, yet no matter how hard she practiced, she had yet to complete a successful experiment on her own.

Her grandfather had given her one experiment to practice. The simple reconstruction of three hyacinth flowers into a potion that could heal wounds. She had collected hundreds since she began practicing, and the flowers had grown quite scarce with all her failed attempts. Though, despite her many failures, she never lost determination. One day, ignoring her grandfather's warnings about the dangers of Neverend, she filled her lungs with courage and set out to the only place where she could still find the flowers, the heart of Neverend. She had made up her mind that she would become a successful alchemist and nothing was going to stop her from reaching that goal.

She wore her favorite blue scarf; it had kept her warm during the chilliest of nights and was the only possession she had left of her parents. It was a reminder to her of that which she had never known. It was a reminder of the mystery that she would one day solve.

That day, Kodi spent many shades seeking the hyacinths but was only able to find two of the vivid purple flowers. She wandered deeper and deeper into the woods seeking the last flower, until all around her started to grow dark.

Keep me warm tonight, mom … dad … wherever you are, she thought while clutching her scarf.

She turned her gaze to the holes in the treetops. The Sun had begun to set and she knew she didn't have much time until the nocturnal creatures of Neverend would come out and about. This had been her first time so deep in the forest, and the fear of darkness crept over her as she stared at the daunting trees that surrounded her from every angle. She took a deep breath, wondering if she should return or remain on her quest. She was on the verge of becoming completely lost. It was then that she heard a loud screech from the distance and what sounded like the shouting of men. Hoping to find someone to aid her back to somewhere familiar, she started running towards the noise.

She found her way to a clearing with little light and came to an abrupt stop, quickly hiding behind a tree. There were voices she could hear clearly. Three of them. Grandpa had always told her to be wary of strangers. She crept around the tree and her eyes fell upon a horrid sight. She watched three men tying ropes around a tiny, black-feathered creature. It was about her size, and looked like an owl except stranger—its eyes, it was something about its eyes.

She tried to get a better glimpse of the unique creature, but a twig snapped beneath her feet and she ducked back behind the tree. She felt her stomach jump into her throat. Closing her eyes, she prayed to Lady Vale that they would not find her. She had a bad feeling in her gut about the men. One of the men, wearing dark brown leather mail, looked up and spoke cautiously.

"Did you hear something?"

One of the others beside him quickened his pace. "Don't get us all riled up," he said. "If a flare shows up, we're done for.

Let's just hurry and get this over with. We'll be so rich, we'll never have to work another day in our lives." Kodi watched the man wipe sweat from his forehead. "Never thought we'd come across a nowl down here. I mean I never even thought I would see one in my life."

Kodi's eyes grew sharp listening to the men. Even at her age she had heard rumors of the poachers who made a living by finding and killing rare animals, then selling parts of their bodies for exorbitant sums. She recalled her grandfather once saying that the feather of a nowl was one of the most valuable items in all of Soria. She turned her focus back to the baby black nowl and could hear its silent whimpering. It was struggling to move but the ropes binding it were too tight. She had to help it. It was what her grandpa would do.

Her mind flooded with a thousand different ideas, each of them too extravagant to work. What could she do? She was just a little kid. Suddenly she stopped, remembering what they had just said. *"If a Kushala shows up, we're done for."*

She flinched as one of the poachers kicked the nowl in the side. "Shut up bird! You'll be dead soon enough anyway so quit your whining." Anger flushed her face. If she didn't know any better, she would have thought the baby nowl was crying. She stared into its eyes; they were a dim orange, as if the life had been sucked from them. They hung half open, a deep look of sorrow coming from within.

This is all I've got, she thought. Reaching to her side, she pulled out a wooden flute with black scales woven around it. She closed her eyes, remembering what her grandfather had said when he bestowed the item upon her.

"This is a special flute, enchanted with the scales of a Kushala Flare. If you're ever in the forest and get attacked, just blow into it." She took a deep breath, placed her lips to the end of the flute, and started to blow.

The second the wind blew through the flute a deafening roar erupted through the forest. Kodi flew back in instant fear, looking around. That was definitely a real Flare. Her eyes glanced all about, trying to find where it had come from.

She quickly placed her back to a tree, hiding. Where would the beast come from … after a second she realized it was completely quiet, and slowly but surely she turned her gaze to the wooden flute in her hands. Wearily, she rotated it slowly between her fingers.

"Did I just do that?" she murmured. Kodi looked forward through the trees to the poachers in the clearing. They had stopped and were frozen dead still. She could hear one of them swearing under his breath. Another one told the other to be quiet. Kodi smiled and took a deep breath, pushing her lips to the flute once again.

Another erupting roar crackled like thunder. She couldn't help but continue smiling as she blew, thinking of her grandfather and his crazy inventions. Of course this would help her. Everything in Neverend was terrified of the Flares, and this special flute, however he made it, could imitate perfectly the ferociousness of their roars. She could hear panicked yelling from the clearing.

"That's definitely a Flare!" One of the men was staring around anxiously. "It's close, too!" He started backing away towards the edge of the clearing.

"What are you doing!?" yelled the leader of the three. "Help me carry this! We'll never have to work another day in our lives with this!"

"No way," muttered the other man. "We shouldn't have messed with this thing! I've heard they're *protected!*" He was now backing towards the edge of the clearing as well.

"I can feel its footsteps!" the man shrieked. Kodi tried not to giggle. Raising her lips one last time, she blew into the flute creating a final terrifying roar that seemed to rattle the trees all around her. Two of the men took off running into the forest. The last man stood for a second, gazing all around before taking off after the other two. Kodi waited several minutes before standing.

Just as she was about to walk into the clearing, a flicker of a shadow through the trees caught her attention. Freezing, she watched as a full grown Flare stalked out into the clearing. She stared up in awe, realizing it was the biggest creature she had ever laid eyes on. Its scales were like midnight and its wolf-like eyes blood red. The small wings on its forearms were tensed, as if it were on edge. She didn't move. She didn't breathe. A feeling that the creature would surely sense her crept into her mind. Her heart skipped as the Flare stalked close to the baby nowl, lying defenselessly. The saliva dripped from its ivory fangs onto the nowl as it stood over it, smelling it.

She didn't know what to do. Tears started streaming down her face. She had never been in a worse situation in her life. This was her fault. A sudden yell echoed from the distance and the head of the Flare whipped in its direction. Instants later it dashed into the clearing of trees toward the sound of the running men. Kodi collapsed to the ground, breathing heavily. Then without thinking, she forced herself to her feet and ran into the clearing.

The baby nowl was whimpering to itself, its wings mangled beneath the ropes. Its breathing was heavy and torn, and she knew it was scared to death of the Kushala. She could see the puddle of blood gathering near its clawed feet from where the poachers had injured it. Cautiously she approached it, scared, but not about to hold back. She slowly reached down and looked into its eyes, "I'm not going to hurt you, ok?" she said as calmly as possible. The nowl screeched loudly as she touched the rope and Kodi jumped back.

"It's ok," she said soothingly. A few moments later she had untied the rope but the nowl still did not move. It was bleeding and its feathers were torn. The light in its eyes was growing dimmer as it watched her, terrified. The puddle of blood it was lying in was thick and seeping through the dirt. She could smell it clearly. It smelt of rust. It had lost too much blood.

Kodi looked at him with saddened eyes. "I'm sorry." She could tell that it would probably never fly again, even if it survived. She sat down next to it and pulled out a piece of bread from her pocket. She held it up before his face, and

XLIV – THE GIRL AND THE NOWL

he hesitated a moment before starting to crunch down on the bread. Slowly, she reached her fingers towards its wing, trying to touch him. The moment her fingers made contact, he turned and snapped his beak aggressively at her.

"Sorry!" she shrieked, caught off guard. "Guess you like to eat in peace …" The nowl watched her intently for a moment before crunching into the bread again. Kodi didn't know what to do. Was she to just leave the nowl here to die? She couldn't carry it back to the cabin, she didn't even know which direction to start walking in. She was completely lost and hopeless. A strong urge to break down and cry overwhelmed her. Everything was wrong. And the worst part was that a real Flare was lurking somewhere close. She slowly surveyed the area, hoping that maybe, just maybe, her grandpa would appear to save her. Then she saw it; a bright purple flower sitting in the distance, all alone.

Her tear-filled eyes grew wide. "That's right! The potion could heal him!" She ran over and pulled the flower carefully from the ground. She closed her eyes as if thanking the flower before turning back to the nowl. She placed three petals on the ground and began drawing a transmutation symbol in the dirt with her finger. She had one chance.

Please work! Her thoughts were racing.

She mentally repeated what her grandfather had told her many times. *"A circle represents the balance and steady flow of power. It must always be perfect."*

Next, she drew a triangle within the circle. *"The triangle is a symbol drawn so that the deconstruction and rebuilding will be contained within the transmutation symbol and kept steady."* Lastly, she drew three circles the size of her fist at each of the triangle's points. *"The last circles are for the specific ingredients. The potion requires three hyacinth flowers, so a simple transmutation circle with a contained and steady balance of power, including three circles for the single triangle's points should be sufficient."*

She steadily placed each of the three petals in the smaller circles drawn at the points of the triangle. Mentally, she coached herself. *Next, I must focus my aura into the transmutation circle and bring it to life. The energy it will take to complete this reaction will take energy from my body. Grandpa told me never to attempt a spell beyond my skill, or the energy taken could drain my entire body and kill me … I've gotta be careful.*

Holding her hands over the center of the circle, she imagined the spell working, the nowl being saved. She could visualize its bleeding stop, and its mangled wings healing. The moment she opened her eyes, streams of blue flame had woven their way out of her palms and into the symbol, bringing it to life. Kodi's eyes lit up. Her heart was racing. She looked at the nowl who was shaking in terror.

"I'm going to save you!" Turning back she took a deep breath. *The last and final step. Understanding what it is that I aim to achieve. I only seek to deconstruct the flowers into their most basic elements, then rebuild them into a new form. A form that I know and understand. I know it'll be more difficult but I'll try using the strengthening incantation to increase the percentage of success.*

Kodi slammed her hands down into the transmutation circle and spoke in a loud clear voice.

"Light of heaven and dark of moon,
Transform these Hyacinths with this tune,
The time has come to bring one care,
Grant me a potion to cure despair!"

She gasped as the flower petals started to glow brighter and brighter. She could feel the energy pulling from her body; it felt as if shackles were chaining down her every muscle and limb and despite her instinctual feeling to pull away she pushed on. The feeling in her fingers grew numb and cold; fatigue came upon her like heavy gravity. Just when she felt she could longer bear it, everything stopped and the light vanished into the shadows. Taking a few deep breaths, she slowly opened her eyes. There before her sat a sparkling purple potion contained by tightly woven vines in the middle of the symbol. The three hyacinth petals were completely gone and the symbol no longer glowed.

"YES!" she cried. "I DID IT!" She grabbed the potion and poured the purple liquid over the nowl's body.

"You're gonna be ok," she whispered, watching in awe as the effects of her potion began transforming the nowl's wounds before her.

He flinched slightly as the liquid steamed over his feathers. Despite how it looked, she was pretty sure that the potion was not hurting the nowl. At least she hoped not. She knelt down as she watched the torn feathers healing and the blood fading, until no signs of the poachers' aggression could be seen at all.

"Amazing ..." she whispered under her breath.

For a second the nowl didn't move. Then in a flash, he was to his feet, watching Kodi carefully.

"There you go," she said with a smile. "You're free."

- - - -

Kodi opened her eyes to see Noctis devouring the last slab of meat. He was enormous compared to that first day. It seemed that he would just never stop growing. That one fateful night in the cold, Noctis had decided to stay with Kodi, and from that moment on they had become best friends.

Kodi turned to the airvras and watched the last of the Enhancers create the smoke rings for the Chasing of the Scarves. A few minutes later, the image switched to the White Castle of Soria. She peered closer as Noctis moved his head down and under her arm. She ran her fingers through the coarse fur behind his ears.

"It's almost time, Noctis."

XLV – The Soldier Games, Begin!

Caim, Storm and Ladon all stared intensely into the airvras. Whatever was projecting the image was flying around the castle, winding through the four great towers and then steadily climbing, higher and higher, circling around the Spearway to Eden. A grand balcony awaited their view at the top, adorned with colorful flowers and hanging green vines. Several trees clad in white bark stood along the edges. Silence fell as the airvras focused in on the white stairs leading up to the balcony.

So she came, walking gracefully up the stairs, her crimson dress swaying ever so softly in the wind, her long white hair falling the length of her body. Everyone outside the coliseum began kneeling. Storm gazed around at everyone in surprise. Even Caim had noticed this and fell to one knee. Storm lowered himself.

Storm snuck a glance at the image projected on the largest airvras. The Empress seemed not much older than him. As the image moved closer he realized that her eyes were the same color as his, with the exception that hers glowed brightly like emerald embers in the night. He felt his cheeks flush, unable to pull his eyes from her. He finally after some time and effort noticed four others at her sides. He stared at the first two soldiers standing beside her. One was enormous, the biggest man he had ever seen, with a thickly bearded face and bright smile, clad in heavy golden armor that shined almost as brightly as his great bald head. His size made the Empress look like a child. To the other side of the Empress was a woman with long silver hair and a stern face; she carried no weapon and was layered in ceremonial feathers and white silk. Upon her left eye was a faded eyepatch.

Storm stared back at the Empress. Why was it that he could not define how he felt about her or what he thought of her? Something about the radiance of the Empress seemed to cage him. She stood alone, as a single star in a blanket of night.

"Is that her?" whispered Caim. Storm froze, hoping nobody had heard. Storm looked over at Ladon but he hadn't budged; it was as if he couldn't drag his eyes away from the airvras. Storm quickly shot Caim a dangerous look and shook his head.

Turning back, he noticed that two more soldiers had appeared behind the Empress. One was a frail-looking man, although he didn't seem old, with long black hair that covered half of his hooded face. At his side he held an enormous black hammer; its head was half the size of the man holding it. Storm wondered how such a frail little man could wield such a beastly weapon.

"That one doesn't look very tough," smirked Caim.

Glancing beyond the frail man, Storm looked to the last of the four. She was a young girl around his age wearing a long white jacket. Placed meticulously above her right ear was a little pink flower, and slung over her shoulder was an ornate white bow; a quiver of arrows hung from her hip. Something about her was familiar. She had a certain fire in her eyes, and her presence reminded him of the deathly chill that had paralyzed his senses earlier, the one that felt mighty as a raging sun. She was a beautiful power.

The Empress approached the front of the balcony. Feeling

a sudden rumbling beneath his feet, Storm realized that cheering was rising across all of Soria. Everyone around him stood, proudly giving the Sorian salute. Cheering grew louder and louder as all the contestants began stamping their feet and weapons. He *had* felt this before. When he was younger he had no idea what it could have been, but now it was clear. It was the past Soldier Games that made the entirety of Soria come alive.

"I've had a crush on her since I was a little boy," Ladon whispered. "How she remains this beautiful after all this time is a mystery to us all. Some believe is has to do with the necklace she wears, which is called Lorienia. Stories say it was given to her by the Goddess of Life." The Empress raised her arms and waved. The rumbling grew even heavier.

"Is she really old?" asked Caim. Storm's eyes darted to his brother.

Ladon nodded his head, unable to avert his eyes from the airvras. "It is only legend, but they say she is one of the *Firstborn*. I've heard also that Grandmaster Arius is one of the Firstborn as well. They are *supposedly* the first and only sons and daughters of Night and Day. She has been around since the very beginning, and has been our first and only Empress. Many stories are told of the necklace Lorienia—you can see it, the crystal pendant around her neck. Some believe it keeps her ageless, while others say that it reflects the beauty of your soul upon your outer beauty. Because she is pure of heart, she has become the most beautiful woman to ever live by wearing it. Or so the legend says." Ladon stopped for a second. "I have only met one other girl in my life that –"

"My dear Soria," the Empress began, and it was as if her voice were speaking within Storm's mind, intimate in a way he could have never anticipated. He stared at Atreyu, realizing that something about the airvras was allowing her to speak to everyone watching.

"We would like to welcome each and all of you to this cycle's Soldier Games. It is soon that the two moons of Aeryx will once again eclipse each other before our sun. The inevitable curve of the ring as some say. We have passed yet again 1000 rings, an entire ten cycles. We have lived once again the memory of Fall, the kindness of Spring, the love of Summer and the loss of Winter. We would ask that all of us take a moment of silence to remember the past … and what we may have lost along the way."

The cheering and rumbling across Soria died. All of the contestants lowered their heads and closed their eyes. Storm closed his eyes. This was truly a changing cycle for him. The overcoming of the old man's challenge. The entering of the Soldier Games. He wondered what their old man would think if he could see them now. A wry smile curved as he imagined the reprimand they would receive.

"We thank you," spoke the Empress, opening her eyes. "Now as always, may we all pluck but one hair from our heads and release it to the wind." Storm watched her reach up and pull one hair elegantly from her head. The strand of white glowed like magic in her fingers. He watched her raise it and let it go, watched as the single strand was swept away. Three of the four warriors next to her did the same. Storm smirked as the giant golden soldier rubbed his sleek, bald head with a hearty smile. Beside him, all of the contestants were following suit. Storm hesitated, watching Caim do the same thing. For a moment the thought of participating in the noble's strange custom infuriated him. Why would he ever have to comply with something like this? Yet despite his anger, something within him caused his hand to reach wearily to his head and pluck a single hair. Looking down at the hair, he stared strangely as the hair changed from black to white in his hand. He released it as if he had been stung.

That was weird, thought Storm. He watched the black sliver of hair be carried off by the wind.

"We can now move forward to the new cycle, for we are no longer the same as we were only a moment ago. The past has not been forgotten, but we have learned and changed as a result of it."

Much to Storm's wonder, several of the contestants around

him had tears in their eyes. The mood of the gathering of warriors had changed drastically. It was as if tearing a piece of them away had allowed them to surpass hindrances of the past that blocked their futures. As if they were cleansing themselves in a spiritual manner.

I can't believe how into this some are, he thought. *It's just a hair ...*

"Once again we stand before you to usher in a new era of brave soldiers. These soldiers come before us, risking everything to fight for something much more important than pride or honor. They fight to become the defenders of our world, the defenders of Life. This, we all know, takes extraordinary courage. A certain bravery that is seldom found ... bravery that is born only in the strong of heart. They are the future heroes of our world. Every day we live ..." The Empress bowed her head low, surprising Storm greatly.

"... We are proud to be among them." The Empress then bowed before them and every contestant kneeled in response. Storm kneeled once again, wondering why a ruler would bow her head to those she ruled. The Empress lifted her head high.

"History cannot be undone. The curves of the ring cannot be foreseen or deterred. Those who fear the future can never move towards it. That is why the Soldier Games are stepping stones. A step towards carving a new history, creating a new world. Yet, as our philosophies state, nothing breeds nothing. Greatness can only be made with sacrifice. That is the reason for the fierceness, danger, and difficulty of the Soldier Games. Only when one is able to risk all can one find the greatness in oneself. Only then can that which was thought to be impossible be born. Sacrifice is unchanging. The ring is unchanging. Yet we must live in a world where we continuously change, adapt and evolve. Perpetual change around that which changes not. Do not fear the future. Strive towards it. And to my dear contestants. Do not fear Death ... for you will meet *him* soon enough."

Storm felt his heart nearly stop. Had she just challenged every single warrior entering the Soldier Games? Had she just proclaimed the deaths of all of them? His fingers tapped on his hilt unwillingly and he stared hard at the Empress. For a split second, it appeared she was staring back at him.

What is it that I am stepping towards? Storm asked himself. *Will I also meet Death one day? I suppose that much is certain. Sacrifice is unchanging. I have sacrificed much to get where I am now. Is she saying that no matter what I do, my path is predetermined? Or is she saying that while one focuses on the pain of the future, you cannot move forward at all? Either way, this feels like a death sentence.*

"Soria is our land. The land we love and that which gives us Life. Granted to us by Lady Vale and the *Children of EIEN*, we have cared for her and thus she has cared for us. Long ago our ancestors took an oath of blood, an oath that became the greatest law of our world. And to this very day, we have borne this oath, through every kind of loss imaginable. Yet, we have never failed our ancestors. Never. We are strong in mind, body and heart. Be you from Risia or Falia, everyone bears the oath of our kind. This oath could not have been possible without each and every one of you ... to those who carry our swords, build our homes, mine our ore, cook our food, raise our children, or even create inventions to help those of the future ... we want to humbly thank you all for your commitment and sacrifices." She bowed her head before raising her eyes and gazing out at the crowd. "For all of you, are heroes in our eyes!" A great cheering erupted again, and the ground beneath them shook tremendously.

"The path may be hard to walk at times, but as long as we all work together, we can create the unbreakable bond that is us! That is ... Soria!!!"

– – – –

Far beyond the bridge Caim and Storm stood upon, beyond the massive gate that separated them from the city of Trestles, hundreds upon hundreds of Falians watched in silence as the Empress delivered her speech. Of the hundreds, two stood in the shadows of the silence, listening and watching. They were Rei and Lucius. They stood in the corner of District Four; where the tent had once been raised, staring at one of two airvras that floated above the white and silver courtyard, lined with many trees along its edges.

At the conclusion of her speech the Empress bowed her head once again. Silence engulfed the courtyard. No one spoke. No one cheered. Only whispers could be heard.

A young man's contemptuous whisper rose above the rest. "How can she say that when she knows that after this cycle, we lose the honor to participate in the Soldier Games?"

"She is a pretender …" answered an older woman with a wrinkled face. "She only pretends to understand that she feels for all of Soria. Heroes in her eyes?" She spit. "The Falians were outcasted many cycles ago. To take away our right to challenge the games is to take away the right to call ourselves sorians! She means to separate the lands and our people … indefinitely."

"Maybe she is right," said a young boy with saddened eyes. "We do not have the strength to protect ourselves anymore. None of Falia has the strength to fight with those of Risia. We would be foolish to pretend that we do. Our pride has been broken, not by our Empress, but by our own weakness! And the inability to learn humility!"

"You know nothing, boy!" shouted another man, but with far less fire in his eyes.

Lucius leaned towards Rei, "I don't see this ending very well …"

"But there *are* strong Falians," she whispered.

Lucius sighed, taking Rei's hand. He knew what she meant. "Yes, they are strong, Rei. But do not pretend. Caim and Storm have condemned themselves. What they seek is impossible. To win the Two Worlds Tournament? They may have power, but we cannot lie to ourselves any longer. They're just kids. They can't hope to compete with *real* soldiers. They are young and reckless and lucky. And, Rei … only for you do I consider this. Even if they win, then what? They broke into the games. They are surrounded by Nobility. They would win only in committing a heinous crime. They will be executed, Rei. But I fear death will come for them much sooner than that." He turned away from her and looked back to the airvras. "I'm sorry, Rei. But they don't stand a chance."

Everything seemed to stop as the truth of Lucius's words crushed her. It felt as if she were drowning in thick heavy wine, suffocated from all sides. Why had she thought that it was possible? She should have stopped them! She should have done anything to stop them! She let them go to their deaths! Tears were filling up behind her eyes but she would not allow them to fall.

"I won't shed tears," she whispered, "for that is the defeat of the body by the heart." She looked up to the airvras. "Even if they are condemned," she began, and Lucius turned away, "I will still have hope."

"Lucius! Rei!" A sudden voice interrupted the both of them. Turning around, Rei looked up to see a tall, muscular boy their age; he had soft and gentle eyes. His left arm and right leg were covered in a terrifying black and dark purple armor; reaching forth from it were sharp claws and a feeling that chilled her bones. Falling from his waist was a crimson half cloak, tattered and worn. She felt a smile crawl over her face.

"Dewey!" Lucius and Rei said simultaneously.

—　　—　　—　　—

Storm sneezed, but no one took notice. The Empress raised her head and was about to speak again.

"We're so proud of all of you. Let these games bring us honorably into a new cycle and continue to drive the determination of our hopes and dreams." She raised her hand high. "Now, without further ado, let us begin the festivities that spark the eve of the new cycle, a new era! The tournament and the birth of new legends ... the 250th Soldier Games!!!"

Storm had to cover his ears from the cheers that erupted around him. Caim, who was normally full of enthusiasm and energy, had a solemn look on his face. He stood there silently as all around him cheered, locked in deep thought.

Storm eyed his brother. *Caim in deep thought?* He imagined Caim and a plus sign with deep thought next to it. *Not possible,* he concluded.

Suddenly, everything became hectic. Many sorians dressed in the same scarlet robes as Arius and Master Atreyu appeared, ushering all of the contestants away from the podium and toward the bridge. Just as Storm was turning to follow the crowd, Caim grabbed his shoulder. His face was surprisingly serious.

"*What*, Caim?" The contestants were rumbling past them, tightening their bracers and holding on to their weapons proudly.

"I figured out the final stage of the Soldier Games."

"Oh yeah?" his voice full of sarcasm. "What's that?'

Caim shook his head. "She said it, Storm. She said we would be meeting Death, soon enough. He'll be there! Death!"

Storm sighed. "I don't think that's exactly what she meant, Caim."

"I'll fight him," said Caim. "*Death.*" His eyes were fiery blue, singing with courage. Storm felt a flicker run through his body, like ice had just run down his back.

"You never change, Caim." Storm laughed. "But don't worry, neo, anything that comes our way … I'll be finishing off before you even get a chance."

Ladon bumped into them, "C'mon, you two!"

"Laboon!" Caim shouted. "I figured out the final stage!"

Ladon stopped and looked back. "What? Stop calling me that!"

Storm pushed Ladon forward, "C'mon," he said. "You said let's go, right?" He shot Caim a warning look, "stop messing around will you?" Caim looked taken aback and didn't walk for a moment. After a second he sighed and followed his brother.

The three of them turned to follow the crowd toward

the edge of the bridge. The side of the coliseum loomed over Storm; its stone was pure white but cracked and dirtied. A faint aura seemed to emanate from it, and for a moment, he wondered if Death really did await them at the end. He watched the wall curve around to the side, the black edge of the bridge inter-joining the wall of the coliseum. Many of the contestants were jumping with confidence up to the edge of the bridge, overlooking the vast blue sky before them. The sun was peeking above the clouds, casting its bright gold rays down upon their silvered armor, veiling them in what Caim felt was the light of luck.

Soon the three of them neared the edge of the bridge, jumped up the thirty feet and stood along its tip. The line of contestants stretched all the way from where the bridge touched the coliseum, and far down past to Storm's left. Each of the contestants had determined looks in their eyes, ready for anything.

"We're about to find out which ribbons we have," said Ladon from Storm's right side. Caim stood to his left. All the contestants were now lined up side by side.

Ribbons? Storm hadn't heard Ladon say anything about ribbons until now. What did ribbons have to do with the beginning of the trial? He peered down over the thick railing of the bridge, a seemingly endless fall beneath them. Storm suddenly remembered this was a flying trial. A tragic thing to forget.

Wonderful.

He glanced out over the empty sky. To his left in the distance, he could see the massive floating land of Falia. He swallowed, gazing at the thousands of green vines hanging from beneath the dark brown cliffs. He looked down. Nothing but sky. He didn't even know if anything existed beneath Soria. Only the tales of Mortal Aeryx existed.

Mortal Aeryx. He could feel his palms starting to sweat, his anger returning. This was Caim's stupid idea wasn't it? How could he compete in this trial? He would be left on the bridge as everyone flew away … embarrassed in front of *both* worlds. He clenched his teeth hard, feeling like they were going to break. Looking forward, Storm was instantly distracted and his mouth opened slightly in confusion. Before him rose a man in black robes with gold trim floating on a cloud. He had long black hair and fierce silver eyes.

The man held up his hands and the whispering stopped. "I am known as Cloud Rider Aurelius, and I will be running each of you through the basics for the Chasing of the Scarves. I would like everyone to take the winged keys from their necks." He held up his own winged key for everyone to see. "Slide the two pieces like this to the side, and your ribbon will be revealed."

Storm's fingers were shaking as he grasped his key. Everyone would see him. He had to fly. He had to do it now. Why was he even scared? He could fly in *Inner Depths*. Nothing made sense. He removed the necklace and held the key in his hand. Sure enough, it looked like it could be split and separated.

Click!

Storm unlocked the key and split the two halves. There, sitting within it, was a tattered white ribbon with the symbol of a grandfather clock in the middle of it. He took out the ribbon and ran it through his fingers. It was soft like silk. No, it felt more like the soft of a feather.

"Oh man, royally sucks to be you mate," he heard Ladon say. Storm looked up to see Ladon looking at Caim's ribbon. It was completely black with a solid yellow lightning bolt in the center. Caim's hands were completely still, unshaking, and Storm clenched his teeth again. How could he be fearless? Maybe he was so stupid he couldn't understand the consequences of anything.

"Cool! A lightning bolt! Wait, what do you mean sucks to be me?" asked Caim.

"Yeah," said Ladon incredulously. "Don't you know what that is?"

Caim shook his head. Ladon looked at Storm. "What, did you two grow up under a rock or something?"

"What'd you say?" said Storm angrily.

"Sorry," said Ladon, backing off. "It's just … that's *Bolt's* ribbon. Everyone knows that, or so I thought."

A girl in leather gloves turned and gazed at Caim with wide eyes, and whispered something to the contestant beside her. Soon, many others were whispering about the ribbon Caim had pulled.

Ladon looked at Caim with stern eyes. "The Chasing of the Scarves is a race, but not just any race. Each contestant must find and catch the scarf with the symbol from your ribbon." Ladon scanned the skies. "Soon they will release the nowls."

Cloud Rider Aurelius continued speaking, "The purpose of this trial is to catch the nowl that is wearing the scarf with the same symbol as your ribbon. They will soon descend past this starting point, guided by the Shepherds—a crew of sorians riding winged Sleipnir–so that they will not fly off course and keep on the path that leads them through the several enchanted rings created by the Enhancers. You, brave contestants, must pursue them, catch the scarf that matches your ribbon from the nowl that is wearing it, and return to the bridge. The first 18 to complete the race are the winners. You should know that once you catch your scarf, you needn't continue the course to finish the race. Just return to the bridge."

Aurelius scanned the contestants grimly. "Upon passing the Enhancement Rings, your keys will activate and pulse against your chest. The choice is yours to activate the enhancement or not. Once you activate the enhancement there are only two ways for it to fade. Make it to the next ring, or break the key. However, the breaking of your key is your forfeit of the Soldier Games. May the light of Vale shine upon you."

Caim raised his hand and Storm nearly fell over, dumbstruck by his brother.

The man cast a look of supreme incredulity. "Yes … my boy?"

"What's a nowl?"

Laughter broke out among the crowd, and several of the contestants patted Caim on the shoulder. Storm could've killed him for his stupidity.

"Ah, the joker," said the man floating on the cloud. His eyes glanced to Caim's ribbon. "And it seems, the bearer of Bolt. A fine sense of humor you have before certain defeat. I wish you the grandest of luck, my unfortunate friend. It seems you had little of that this morning when adorning your armor."

Again laughter broke out. Storm had to admit that Caim did look ridiculous. Caim just shrugged.

"So, is someone going to tell me what Bolt is?" Caim said to Ladon.

Ladon looked grim. "Sorry, Geoerge ... but that ribbon means ..." He looked away. "It means you've already lost."

"What!?" Caim cried. "I don't want this ribbon! I want to try at least!"

"Oh, well you'll get to *try*. It's just ... no one has ever caught Bolt. He's the fastest nowl in all of Soria. Why do you think his symbol is lightning?"

Storm looked at his own ribbon. A grandfather clock was his symbol. Did that mean he had the slowest nowl in all of Soria? He smirked at Caim. *Serves you right with your unfaltering courage,* he thought. *Let's see you catch that which cannot be caught.*

"Oh, good!" said Caim brightly. "I thought I wasn't allowed to play the game."

"Play?" said Ladon. "You know thousands have died in this challenge right?"

"I know," said Caim. "But not me. I won't die. Not here."

"How could you possibly know that?" asked Ladon.

Caim gave Ladon a thumbs-up. "Because I know." He squeezed the ribbon in his fist. "I'll definitely catch him. The Dragon King would catch him, and so will I."

Storm watched a stupefied look take over Ladon's face upon Caim's mention of the Dragon King. It was as if he'd just been told the lands of Soria weren't floating, or that the

Curseborn were rulers of Nobility.

"And now," said Cloud Rider Aurelius, "we will be releasing the nowls and starting the race. Remember, no one is to move until the last nowl has passed the bridge, and the light in the cloud turns green!"

Shit, thought Storm.

He felt his stomach churning. He looked to Caim, who was staring out at the sky, calmly waiting. An involuntary sense of revulsion rose within him, and for a moment he wanted Caim to lose. "Looks like you won't be moving to the next race, neo." Caim didn't move or turn, and his disregard angered Storm further.

He closed his eyes and tried to center himself. *Ok, this won't be that bad, I've flown in Inner Depths ... I can do it here. I will not be left alone on this bridge!*

Storm warily opened his eyes and looked down. He instantly felt like he was spinning and the fall was inevitable. He closed his eyes again, but even in his thoughts he could see the fall. *I will not lose here!* He chided himself. *Not like this!* Why couldn't this challenge be a fight? *Stupid Nobles ...* What was the point of chasing a stupid scarf? He felt like ripping his hair from his head.

"It's in your head neo. I know you know that." The voice was practically smirking at him and his temper flared hot like molten steel.

Storm turned his eyes to the source of the words directed at him. *Caim.* His brother's words were full of a taunting energy that made Storm feel like ripping his sword from his sheath and slicing off Caim's smart tongue. He shook his head at the violence of his own thought.

"They're coming ..." Ladon spoke, his neck arched back. Storm followed Ladon's eyes, peering into what seemed like an empty sky. He squinted and far in the distance, something came into view. Specks littered the sky like black stars. They grew larger and larger until they came into focus.

Hundreds and hundreds of nowls zoomed through the air. They cut the wind like blades as they hurtled past each other, hooting loudly. Out to their flanks were several sorians riding Sleipnir; they looked of winged horses, but with six legs, and their manes were long and flowed like liquid silver from their backs. Their wings flapped powerfully as they tried to keep pace. The nowls zoomed past the Shepherds, coming inches away from them, before barreling back towards the tip of the coliseum.

Storm gasped, his fears vanishing for a moment. The flock soon reached the top of the coliseum, flying inches from its outer wall. Spinning and shooting past one another, they reached the bridge. Storm froze. The nowls were enormous. Their eyes were like shining jewels, large and round and full of intelligence. He felt like they understood him while he made eye contact, and for that single moment, everything evaporated but the connection between them. And then like the snapping of a twig, they were gone with the wind.

"They're *fast!*" said Caim, trying to keep his balance as they rocketed past. "This is going to be awesome!!" He turned to look at Storm. "You can do it Storm! Get out of your head and just let go!" A grin curved across his face. "I know you can." Storm narrowed his eyes.

"Or maybe you can't," said Caim, and stuck out his tongue. He raised his arms and roared as loudly as he could to the skies, "Either way I'm catching Bolt!!!" His roar was followed by the loudest battle cry Storm had ever heard. All the contestants were roaring now.

Storm wanted to yell at him but he didn't. The tension on the bridge was rising. Everyone was bracing themselves. He stared out at the cloud the man sat on. Above it three jewels came to life. They sat horizontally next to one another, separated only by bits of cloud. The leftmost was red, the second yellow, and the last green. Storm felt his heart freeze as the red one illuminated.

"This is it," he muttered under his breath. Lightning was surging through his body.

The yellow jewel illuminated next. The contestants readied themselves.

I will not be left alone! Storm fidgeted his boots and found his grip. He flexed both fists and leaned forward, gazing out at his fear. *I will not be defeated by this. I am more than this!* His lips curled into a grin, feeling his elation devouring his fear.

The green jewel lit up. A huge bang echoed across Soria. Storm felt a hurricane of wind as all the contestants launched themselves into the air, spreading their arms and falling away from him. He felt like he was falling backwards as their auras burst from their bodies like flames.

He stood alone.

XLVI – Chasing of the Scarves

The pressure of the contestants leaving the bridge nearly toppled Cloud Rider Aurelius from his floating cloud. Their auras formed around their bodies in all different colors; some flew with deep green auras while others had light blue or even orange ones. They all looked of flames, growing and twisting from their cores, as if their spirit had been set aflame and become tangible energy; their ambitions had taken form.

Caim took off from the edge of the bridge into the air. He hadn't flown in a while and laughed with delight. He could feel the wind on his face, and closed his eyes. There was nothing like flying. Nothing at all. Only when he was flying was he completely free, unchained by all the shackles of life, free to go anywhere his heart desired.

But not this time. This time he was not free. His eyes flashed open, focused on the flock of nowls, and with a burst of power, Caim shot into the far reaches of the sky.

Back on the bridge, one lone contestant stood still, draped in shadows, watching as the others flew off into the distance after the flock of fast-moving nowls. He stood in unwieldy silver armor with a sour look upon his face; his fists were clenched tightly at his sides.

"This is so *damn stupid!*" Storm yelled.

Trying to look for Caim, Storm felt his foot slip and his stomach jumped into his throat. A sudden visceral feeling alerted him to an unknown presence—someone, or something, was watching him. He turned and found it.

About ten feet away, a single nowl, easily twice his size, stared at him through squinted eyes. Astonishingly, the nowl wore a monocle, held by a silver chain that wrapped around its neck.

Storm surveyed the mysterious creature. It was old and white with tattered feathers, and had many small brown spots on its puffed out chest. Under its beak was a long, thin and white braided beard, reaching nearly three feet from its chin. On the top of its head was a tiny puff of silver hair that looked like it might blow off with a single gust of wind. But none of that surprised Storm more than the fact that sitting within its mouth was a long thin pipe with little circular rings of smoke rising from the end of it.

"You have got to be kidding me," Storm muttered. He turned to see the flock of nowls growing smaller in the distance. "I don't have time to be messing with you," he said. "See those stupid birds in the distance?" The nowl twisted its head. "That's where I need to be."

"*Hoot!*" replied the nowl.

Just as Storm was about to lunge at the nowl to chase it off, he saw something that made his jaw drop. Wrapped around the nowl's neck was an old white scarf, and smack dab in the center of it was the symbol of a grandfather clock.

Storm grinned wickedly. He couldn't believe his luck—he didn't even have to fly to catch his nowl! He moved forward along the edge of the bridge until the nowl was just within his grasp, but just as he was about to close his fingers on its scarf, it flew off. He swung to the side to see the nowl floating a few feet off the side of the bridge.

"Just give me your scarf, and no one gets hurt." The nowl

turned its back to him and started fluttering its way towards Falia, just far enough from the bridge so Storm could not reach him.

"Really!?" He started dashing along the side of the bridge, but his speed was hindered by the fat noble's armor. High above him Storm could sense the presence of one of the sorian shepherds. And then he heard it, a voice that all of Soria could hear—the voice of the Announcer.

"Kicking off the start of the Games, it looks like we have a straggler down here! This one's running across the edge of the bridge, folks—what could he be thinking!?"

Storm picked up his speed, hoping to outrun the nowl. Minute after minute he hobbled as fast as he could, and even though he could tell the nowl was slower than others, his running speed was nothing compared to the speed of flying. He soon passed the massive twisting stairs that led to the coliseum's entrance; past the dozens of grand statues built along the bridge's edge; past the many tents and shops that were set up, waiting for the entry of the crowd. He hated this feeling of being constantly watched. He knew the Announcer was following him—his futile pursuit of the nowl was being seen by everyone in Soria. He cursed out in despair as the nowl neared the end of the bridge and rose higher.

"Let's see here," said the Announcer. "He seems to be chasing his nowl, by foot. Yes, that is correct, ladies and gents, his nowl has flown off course and is headed straight for the city of Trestles!" Storm tried to block out the announcer's voice. It did not work.

"Wait, what's this? I'm getting a clearer view of this particular nowl. It seems that the nowl chosen for this poor contestant is none other than one of Soria's legends, a favorite of favorites! Yes, to all who have been waiting for him, it is the great nowl Einstein! Despite a speed that rivals the crawling of a newborn, this nowl has only been caught once in the history of the Soldier Games, and by our very own Lady Sakura of the Force Corps! A true nowl among nowls, Einstein uses his superior intelligence to avoid capture. Will our young contestant find what it takes to bring him down!? I'm sure we'll find out soon—that is, if he ever gets off his feet and starts flying!"

Storm had his fists clenched up in front of his face. He didn't know whether to take out the announcer or continue chasing the nowl. *Just calm down*, he coached himself. *There's no point to this if I don't catch the stupid bird. I lucked out. Even the announcer said he's slow. Now I just have to catch him.*

Storm soon cleared the jump to the top of the great black gate and entered the town of Trestles. It was now more than ever that he felt the heavy silver armor holding him back. In sudden spontaneity, he thrust the heavy silver helmet from his head, and heard it *clank* on the stone ground. Instantly he felt better, and pulled his hood over his head.

Next he tore off his breastplate and tossed it. Next came the greaves, until all he chose to keep were the silver bracers. If he got caught, so be it. But unless they saw the mark on his wrist, there was little chance, especially with the bracers concealing it. He had seen other nobles dressed without armor during Arius' speech. *As long as I have this white paint on my Hollow and the bracers, I don't think anyone will notice, especially since most of the contestants weren't wearing heavy armor like this.*

He dashed through crowds of Falians who cheered for him, which made his cheeks flush with embarrassment, and leapt from rooftop to rooftop, quickening his pace. In the distance he could see Einstein floating over the shops towards District Two, several rings of smoke floating just above him. It looked as if he were heading towards the exit of the city and towards the lake that led to the edge of Neverend.

Trying to escape to the forest, ka? The only sound he heard was several *hoots* as Einstein continued flying over Trestles.

"You'll never catch him!" shouted one of the Falians. Storm turned to cast him an evil glare—and almost smashed into a family. The mother of the three young children glared at him contemptuously.

"Shut it!" he cried, flashing past them. His eyes sought Einstein and found him in the distance. He jumped up to a rooftop and flashed a hundred feet farther to another. "I'm gonna pummel you when I catch you!"

Storm leapt from a final rooftop and landed in the initial

courtyard of Trestles, the black fountain flashing past him as he ran. He nearly collided with a young girl who ran in front of him. "DON'T STEP ON THE FLOWERS!" she screamed. His eyes jumped back at her, but it wasn't Rei. Turning back, Storm jumped straight over the flowers and kept running. His eyes focused on Einstein just before he lost sight of him. He watched Einstein disappear over the outer wall of the city. Faster now that he was lighter, Storm dashed towards the entrance, and with one last movement, exited through the colossal entrance gates of Trestles.

—   —   —   —

Caim dodged his way through the speeding contestants, a bright smile curving across his face as he made his way steadily to the front of the pack. The biggest contestants were by far the slowest, and he had long since passed them. The girls, on the other hand, were lighter in frame and Caim had difficulty keeping pace with them. In the far distance something caught his eye. As he neared it, his vision became focused. Floating in the air was a large black nowl who had stopped racing; the feathers on its head rose like a spiked midnight mane, running all the way down its back. The fur around its face was black except for two patches of white that covered its eyes. The creature had a powerful presence.

A mask? Caim thought, staring at the white patches around its eyes. The nowl was hovering in the air, glaring at him. Caim's eyes widened as he saw the scarf around its neck—all black with a vibrant yellow lightning bolt in the center.

"It's you!" he cried, coming to a halt in the air. He could feel the vibrations as the other contestants passed him at ridiculous speeds, some nearly smashing into him. After a few moments, it was only Caim and the black nowl locked in a stare-down.

"So you're the one that no one ever catches, huh? Don't look very fast to me. Look pretty stupid actually." Caim placed his hands on his hips and laughed. "You shouldn't have stopped in the middle of the race, stuuupid nowl! Ha-ha! Now you are mine!" The nowl raised his wing and made a motion to brush dirt off its shoulder. Caim's eyes sharpened. "Think you can taunt me and get away with it!?"

High above them the announcer came to a stop above them. "The moment we've been waiting for, everyone! The fastest nowl in all of Soria, the only nowl to have never been caught has made his appearance! Let's have a grand welcome to the nowl we all know and love! Please welcome Bolt back to this cycle's Soldier Games!!!"

Bolt folded one wing under his muscular frame and bowed. Caim stared perplexed at the announcer in the sky. He rode upon a white-winged Sleipnir with a majestic golden mane.

"It seems like only yesterday that Bolt flew circles around the contestant of the last games all the way to the finish line without ever getting touched once. My, oh my, how embarrassing that must have been! Well, we all know Bolt knows how to bring the heat, and today folks, he isn't letting us down! Coming to a dead stop and taunting this new contestant. He really knows how to get under their skin! Wait! What's this!? The contestant is flying this way!"

Caim came to a stop before the Announcer, glaring at the young man with long white hair and hazel eyes. He wore a cut off black vest, and tattoos ran down the length of both arms. Caim stretched out his finger and pointed at him. "You shut your mouth!"

The Announcer shot him a smirk and flashed his white teeth, a red bandana rippling around his neck in the heavy winds. The fiery eyes of the flying white steed glared at Caim, as if warning him of being too close. "Now, now, young eager one," began the announcer, "this is no time to be worrying about me. At this very moment, Bolt is—by the Empress's name, he's right behind you!"

Caim whipped around, his nose almost touching the tip of Bolt's beak. "Stupid bird!" he said, flashing his hand out to grab the scarf. He could feel it on the tip of his fingers before it vanished before his eyes.

The bird was *fast*. Caim looked up to see Bolt floating above him, upside down. Bolt brought his wing up and taunted Caim again. Caim's entire body quivered with anger.

"Oh, now you're going to get it!!!" screamed Caim.

Bolt flew in the direction the other nowls had headed. Caim placed his arms to his sides, and steadily increased his speed until he felt he couldn't fly any faster. Just as he thought he was inching close, Bolt would accelerate and gain a huge distance on him. How could he be so fast? Coming up in the distance, Caim could see the first Enhancement Ring. Flashes of the old man blowing smoke filled his thoughts. He couldn't remember what Laboon said they did. The ring came into focus—an enormous smoky circle laced with vibrant blue aura. It wasn't long before Bolt soared through the ring and Caim, close behind, followed through it.

He suddenly felt the winged key pulse on his chest and remembered. *That's right! All I have to do is click the wings together and—*

Click!

Caim came to a halting stop. "What the ..." He could barely speak. He felt as if all the weight of the world had been added to his body. His fingertips now weighed more than his entire body. A crushing pressure engulfed his every strength, forcing him downwards. He could barely manage to keep himself up in the air and his speed fell to a deathly crawl.

"What ... is ... this!?" he managed to say, struggling to keep afloat. He could hear the voice of the announcer who was clearly not going to stop following the crowd's favorite attraction. Caim looked to his arms and legs; twirling around them was a thick brown aura that looked like snakes with crimson eyes. Wrapped around their bodies were thick silver bands, many of them. They looked enormously heavy.

"Oh and what a turn of bad luck!" cried the announcer. "It seems our contestant has received the negative status effect known as Landfill! Oh my, what a wicked turn of events. I can't believe he's still flying! Landfill, as most of you know, increases the weight of your body by 50 times! What ever will he do!?"

"50 TIMES MY WEIGHT!?" cried Caim as Bolt flew around him in circles. He watched angrily as Bolt flew up right next to his face and began tapping him on the head with his wing. "You ... are seriously ... going to ... get it," though Caim could barely speak. He could feel his head getting heavy and his body beginning to ache terribly. The effect was like chains shackling him to whatever darkness awaited beneath him. For all he knew, it was an endless fall to Mortal Aeryx—the land of eternal darkness.

This was bad—he wouldn't be able to fly much longer at all. He gulped as he stared at the empty sky beneath him. "Not like this ... not like this!" he swore loudly, sinking downwards. There was nothing he could do, nothing at all. It was a weight far worse than the ten times gravity training they had endured in their grandfather's *Inner Depths.*

The announcer and his steed swept down from the sky. "Oh no! The contestant has begun to fall! It seems that we will witness the most unfortunate of events. The first death of this cycle's Soldier Games is nigh upon us! Please, let all of us cheer on this brave contestant!!!"

Caim's mind grew blank as he lost all feeling in his arms and legs. He was now tumbling through the air, legs over his head, arms flailing to the sides. No power remained. Despite his most strenuous attempts, his body had become useless. Even his eyelids felt like they weighed a thousand pounds. It felt as if Soria itself were sitting on top of him, forcing him down, condemning him. Faster and faster he twisted downwards, unable to move, unable to breathe. He closed his eyes. He heard his grandfather's voice and found himself smiling.

"The moment before you die is the moment you understand what kind of man you are."

Storm's grinning face appeared in his mind next, followed by his words. *"You're really going to let this stupid little bird defeat you? I know I wouldn't be defeated by such a thing. Who are you, Caim?"*

Caim clenched his fists, tightening his knuckles until it felt like his bones would snap out of his fist. The wind was ripping across his face but he could barely feel it any more.

Who am I? Everything was dark. He could no longer open his eyes. Only within could he see. And only darkness was found. *I am a brother. I am a swordsmen. And I …"* A faint light grew clearer in the darkness. *And I …* He soared towards the light. *I am stronger than this!*

And then his mind focused on a flame. A rippling white flame within, surging with the unrelenting power of a sun. Wearily he reached towards the flame. He could feel the cage within his body that held his aura cracking and ripping apart. He then screamed as loud as he possibly could.

"I AM GOING TO WIN THE SOLDIER GAMES!!!"

Caim's aura exploded out of his body in a flash of bright white energy. Slowly, he came to a stop in midair, his eyes sharp and his expression enraged. His limbs felt like they were being ripped apart from his body, but he did not fall another inch. With terrible effort, Caim began ripping the armor of the noble from his body. They fell one by one to the unknown depths, never to be seen again.

"I can't," he spit, "I won't lose to a stupid bird!" Caim forced everything he had—all his focus, all his energy—into flying. Slowly but surely, he began to inch his way upwards in the sky. Far off in the distance something caught his eye. It was the second Enhancement Ring. It was far. But not unreachable. A beacon of hope.

Caim coughed and blood trickled down his lips. The strain on his body was overwhelming; as if a shadow of death hovered ominously over his shoulder, peering its sunken skull-like face next to his, grinning its wicked and horrible grin. Waiting for him to let go. All he had to do was let go.

"Ladies and gents, I can't believe my eyes!" the announcer shrieked. "The competitor has pulled himself out of what looked like a hopeless fall and now moves toward the second

Enhancement Ring! By the Empress's name, people, his spirit! Will he make it!? He's … he's …" The announcer choked. "Oh, it's horrendous! Wounds are ripping open on his arms and legs … he's leaving a trail of bloody aura in his wake. I can't bear to watch this any longer."

Caim could hear an outburst of cheering from across Soria. The lands were coming alive, fighting beside him. He felt a huge gash rip open on his chest, and the warmth of crimson seep down his sides. "I'll make it. I won't die here. No matter what!!!"

He could feel his energy draining fast and tried to erase the thought from his mind that he actually might not make it. Everything around him grew hazy, as if he were drowning in perfectly clear water. He could see, yet everything was fuzzy, fading, becoming distant. Somehow he pushed forward, unaware of how it was happening. All he knew was to move forward. There was nothing else. Nothing more. Yet a faint awareness stalked the back of his thoughts, and he knew that if the next ring didn't grant him some change of luck, his energy would be sure to …

No!!! His thoughts screamed and raged and fought against every bit of doubt.

"There is only one option," he screamed. "I will die!"

XLVII – Camouflage

C'mon Noctis, let's go!" called Kodi, pulling herself onto his
back. It was a high climb, and he squawked as she grasped
tightly to his coarse fur. Once finding her little place between
his shoulder blades, she laid herself flat. Her black leather
clothing and the blue scarf wrapped around her head made
Noctis look exactly like the nowls flying in the games.

"Head down to the caves," she whispered in his ear.
Noctis extended his wings and with one giant thrust they
rose up into the air. Noctis dove down past the edge of Soria,
scaling the cliffs as close as he could without running into
their sharp edges. Kodi took a deep breath as she looked
down, watching as they soared along the edge of the floating
land, diving faster and faster down its side. Her heartbeat
raced as they flew. "I forgot how much I love flying with
you!" she shouted. Noctis merely replied with a *hoot*. He cast
his wings out, cutting his speed in half and flew straight past
many hanging vines. He passed suddenly into a dark cave.

Kodi took in a full view of her surroundings. The cave
was dark and treacherous; thousands upon thousands of sharp
stalactites hung from the ceiling. Water dripped into large

puddles from their tips, and she knew that the water was coming from the many rivers of Falia. The cave was not too wide yet big enough for even a Chameleoth to fly through. Shadows flitted out of the corner of her eyes as the droplets of water echoed eerily. They flew in silence, Kodi taking in the surroundings, seeking a suitable place to hide. She had only been here once before, to prepare her plan. Though at that time it had been nighttime and even harder to see anything. At the farthest end of the cave she could see a faint light, the other entrance. Despite the light, she knew the distance across was incredibly far. Although it spanned a distance that was not the widest area of Falia, it was still a cave that reached from the northern edge to the southern.

"I heard the entrance to the Thousand End Caves could be found somewhere down here," she said softly to Noctis. "I wonder if they even exist. Grandpa said that only in entering myth could one find the Thousand End Caves. Whatever that means …"

She pointed ahead to a dark area where an enormous rock icicle had shattered on the ground, creating an uprising of rocks, each bigger than Noctis. "Let's hide behind those." Noctis landed softly on the ground, and Kodi slid down his back, stepping in a massive puddle.

"Ugh!" She shook her boots. "I knew something like this was going to happen. What a way to start." She cautiously reached around, touching the surprisingly warm stone. "I wonder why these are so warm …" She ran her fingers across the shattered stalactite. "That's odd. I'll have to investigate later."

Peering around their hiding spot, she pointed to the faint light at the end of the cave. "Alright Noctis, that's where they are going–" She froze and turned to find Noctis with a cave rodent in his mouth. And then it was gone. Swallowed whole. "Will you pay attention!?" Her voice echoed unexpectedly and she froze.

She switched to a whisper. "Will you pay attention?" Noctis lowered his head, focusing his eyes on her. "Thank you. Now, at the far end of the cave is where they are going to enter. Remember Noctis, at this point the contestants should be catching up to them, so we have only one chance." She held up one finger. "One. Chance. Got it?" Noctis made a deep purring sound. "No, I will not pet you right now. I'm nervous about this. If we get caught, I'm the one that's going to get executed because *you* are a celestial creature." Noctis cocked his head. "Don't give me that look," she retorted. "To you I may be a celestial creature, but to them I'm just a damned Curseborn."

For many minutes Kodi and Noctis waited silently. Every few minutes she had to turn around to hush him, for in the aging of nowls, Noctis was relatively young. He had a problem with keeping his attention focused. After what felt like nearly a shade of waiting and when the dampness of her boots had become utterly unbearable, she heard something in the distance.

"Shh! I think they're coming." A second later she turned around with bright eyes. "They're coming!" Noctis leaned down and Kodi jumped up his back, this time much faster than the first. "Ok Noctis, you know what to do … don't get caught!" He arched his back in a proud and irritated manner. "Seriously Noctis, you need to focus. Yes, my feet are wet too. I know you hate that. It's not fun for me either."

Kodi tucked her head against his feathers. The sound of hooting and the flapping of wings grew louder and louder as the minutes passed. There were even slight moments of silence where Kodi held her breath, wondering if something had happened to delay them and that this whole effort might be wasted. And then she saw one, a completely aqua-colored nowl wearing a red scarf. It shot past them, dodging the hanging stalactites with ease. And then another. And then four others. And then many others. Soon, the cave had become filled with the flapping of wings and the hooting of nowls zooming past one another, as if they were merely playing a game.

"Your family is beautiful," whispered Kodi, "but I

wonder if they're faster than you?" Noctis blew hot air from his nostrils and with one step launched into the air, accepting the challenge. Within seconds Noctis was soaring alongside other nowls who turned suspicious eyes towards Kodi. They knew that she was riding on an outsider. Several of them surrounded Noctis, flying at high speeds, testing him with their prying eyes.

"Please," said Kodi. "We mean you no harm." She stared into their eyes deeply, pleading with them. With one final glance, the other nowls took their attention from Noctis and flew towards the end of the cave. Kodi released a nervous breath and turned her head to look behind them. The contestants weren't far behind. Some were running along the ground, others running along the walls, and some attempting to fly through the sharp icicle graveyard.

"They'll come upon us soon enough. Hopefully, our scarf doesn't look like any of the ones they're chasing or this is going to end horribly."

It wasn't long before the flock of nowls exploded out of the side of the cave, coming into the sky like a blur of weaving colors. It would have been an incredible sight to see, were Kodi not sitting right in the center of it. Immediately, she could feel the presence of the shepherds above.

"Noctis, I was right in assuming they can't enter the cave! The Sleipnir are powerful but they're not agile enough to keep pace with the nowls in such a dangerous area. They were forced to fly above Falia, waiting for the nowls to emerge from the other side." Noctis stayed close to the other nowls, camouflaging himself as best he could. Kodi closed her mind, attempting only to think of herself as a nowl, and no more.

She peeked upwards as they passed through one of the smoky rings, grateful that she had no winged key around her neck. She knew the horrifying enchantments were often more detrimental than helpful. After a moment, she laid her head back down on Noctis's back. It wouldn't be long before they reached the end of this mission and began their real one.

She looked at her black gloves and the symbols etched upon them.

On her left glove, a complex transmutation symbol carved in crystal—the Alkahest. The universal solvent, the ultimate tool of deconstruction. The ability to return anything to its base property. She looked at her right glove; woven into the top of it was a glowing rosy gem staring ominously back at her. A near complete Philosopher's Stone. The ultimate tool of reconstruction. The stone of rebirth. She grasped Noctis's fur tighter. With these tools of Alchemy she could do it.

"I'll find your book, grandpa," she said aloud. "I promise!"

XLVIII – A Shimmer of Emerald and Crimson

Storm kept his eyes peeled for the obnoxious little nowl named Einstein. He had been led across the long black bridge, through the white courtyards of Trestles and past the glistening lake that sat just beyond its outer gates. He was now in Neverend. Not even close to the course he should have been on. Racing through the trees, Storm could only follow by listening to the occasional *hoots* he faintly heard. He knew exactly why the nowl was leading him into the forest. With so much cover from trees, he would be nearly impossible to find. Despite his various attempts at a plan, he had yet to think of any that might work. He was betting on the sole fact that Einstein would be overly confident, considering he had only been caught once.

Storm ran into a clearing and came to a skidding stop. "Where are you?" he muttered, looking around. The couple hundred-foot-tall trees rose at the clearing's edge, seemingly bending towards him, trying to obstruct his view and hinder his progress. The smell of sap was stronger here than in other places and the clearing had a familiar feeling that he recognized at once. Hundreds of leaves once full of life had fallen and blanketed the grass around him.

From his position, it felt like Einstein was leading him north through the forest, not east, the direction from which he and Caim had traveled. Storm walked toward a grey bark tree standing in the center of the clearing; it was taller than the rest with leaves a dark hazelnut brown clinging to life on the ends of branches. He looked closely at the curving roots; resting among them was a flat stone. There, on the single flat stone was a transmutation circle carved in blood; his blood, and sharp fragments of emerald.

Skipping stones, he thought with a coy smile.

His gaze rested on the stone and he wondered if anything Rei had said from the Alchemy shop could really be true—it seemed unlikely that the power she said the stone contained was real. Alchemy was a completely different kind of skill than what he was accustomed to. Train harder, get stronger. Not memorize hundreds of different patterns and look for rare gems with *hidden* power. The sudden hooting of Einstein brought Storm back to reality. Looking to the treetops, Einstein was nowhere in sight.

Maybe I can't see you from down here, he thought, looking back at the grey tree. *But from up there* ... Storm leapt up the twenty feet to the first branch with ease. Flipping himself from branch to branch, he quickly made his way to the top. Scanning the horizon of bushy treetops, he could feel his palms starting to sweat again. *This is getting really annoying,* he thought. His eyes scanned steadily over the endless trees.

He squinted at the distant horizon. Black clouds were rolling inwards, darker than Night herself. They were far but moving fast, and he wondered if the storm would reach Falia by the end of the day. Above him, the gleaming orb of fire was making her way into the center of the sky, sitting above a fortress of shifting clouds, with lances of golden light piercing the canopy of trees. He could see nothing but the green and brown leaves, some darker, some lighter. It was then that his eyes fell upon something strange. One of the lances of light was reflecting something; a tiny white puff that seemed out of place not too far from where he stood.

"I know that little puff, you dirty little bastard," said Storm under his breath. "I've got you now." He crouched down and leapt in the direction of the hiding nowl. However, Einstein had been watching him and as soon as Storm dashed in his direction, he took flight from the trees.

"I'm not about to let you get away!" Storm jumped up and across the tops of the trees faster and faster. Ducking branches and flashing through trees, he sped towards the rising nowl. Tiny creatures with long floppy ears vanished into tiny holes in the tree trunks as he passed like a blur of black. He was gaining on him. Yet it seemed that no matter how fast he ran he couldn't quite close the gap.

He wondered how the race was going for others as this stupid nowl led him all around Neverend. Storm ran and ran, minute after minute, until he felt like he wasn't making any progress at all. Every time he tried to lunge at the nowl through the treetops, he was just barely off, or too low. Einstein was taking advantage of the fact that he couldn't fly, exploiting Storm's greatest weakness. It wasn't long before Einstein descended into another clearing ahead of them that seemed to open up and out of the forest. Storm flipped himself one last time, landing on a thick branch, and stopped dead in his tracks, his eyes widening as he stared into the clearing.

"You have got to be kidding me right now!!" he shouted, then quickly cupped his hands over his mouth.

The clearing was no clearing at all. It was the gap between the two great forests of Falia; the magical forest of Neverend and the sky reaching forest of Ravenia. Enormous rocks that shone of silver littered a clay-covered basin that made Storm feel that a monstrous mountain would rise up beyond them. Past the boulder-strewn clearing he could see the black and silver trees of Ravenia and he shuddered at the thought of the ghostly place.

Air sprayed with dirt sifted through the clearing, bringing a rancid smell that smarted Storm's senses. He immediately covered his nose. In the center were four of the biggest stones, piled together like tombstones, and lying against one another at diagonal angles. Basking on these four silvery tombstones were four creatures of midnight might. Four full grown Flares soaking up the sunshine.

Storm stifled a cry. Could this really be happening? Not one, but *four Kushalas*!?

Their black leathery scales stretched along their half-wyvern, half-wolf bodies, reaching down their backs. Their spiked serpentine tails waved calmly, some twitching, others unmoving. They stretched their claws, tensing and un-tensing the rippling black wings that lay on their forearms like elbow bones that had grown too far. Silently, he crouched down, surveying their black chests, wondering if the Master of the Forest was among them. He searched for the silver mark and couldn't find it. Storm felt a massive weight fall from his shoulders. Yet the one sitting on the largest tombstone was enormous, rivaling the size of the Master of the Forest. It was then he found Einstein.

"Now how did you go and manage that," muttered Storm.

Sitting on the biggest Kushala's head was Einstein. How the Kushala had not noticed, he did not know. Maybe it just didn't care. He shook his head. Maybe if there was one, he could defeat it. But there were four. And even if he could somehow, miraculously, fight all of them off, the race would be well over by the time he was finished.

He swore under his breath, watching as Einstein, who never seemed to stop smiling through squinted eyes, puffed away on his little wooden pipe. Storm watched the circular rings rise into the air. What was the purpose in wearing a monocle if his eyes looked as if they were constantly closed? Storm grimaced—was he really trying to figure out why this bird was wearing a monocle? He sat perfectly still for a few minutes before noticing something else enter the clearing.

Straight through the upper lining of trees behind the beasts, a single airvras floated in above them all, and then he heard it. A voice that brought him true irritation.

"Ladies and gentlemen! It seems that Einstein has led his contestant straight into the midst of a Kushala Den! And not just that, but he has somehow perched himself upon the biggest Kushala Flare's head I've ever seen! As you can all see, our contestant stands hiding in the branches of the trees, clearly having met his match with this nowl! Things are looking bad for this *flightless* one. What ever will he do!?"

Storm took several deep breaths, deeply resisting the urge to run out and destroy the airvras. He couldn't see the announcer, but sensed that he was nearby. He had to think of something now. Time was ticking and he was getting nowhere.

I'm going to catch you and swing you by that ridiculous white beard of yours around and around until you ... Storm shook his head. *Focus. This is getting nowhere.*

If I can just alert them to the stupid bird on its head, they'll take him down for me. He grinned evilly. *Little bastard, serves you right.* He looked around for something to throw. It would have to be a perfect throw. One chance. He found a short but sturdy branch and reached forward; he wrapped his fingers around it easily and snapped it off.

CRACK!

A sudden presence of bloodlust enveloped his senses. He turned cautiously. Four pairs of glaring crimson eyes met his gaze. He gulped. Their tails were twitching eagerly, the putrid smell of venom growing stronger. He could hear their growling like the coming of an earthquake. Storm could feel his eyes starting to water.

The biggest Kushala stood to its feet, Einstein still sitting calmly on its head. Even the trees seemed to flinch as it roared loudly. Slowly, the other three stood to their full might as well.

"If it isn't Black Rains." Storm heard the voice of one of the Kushala speak into his mind. *"And he's alone this time. It would seem luck has graced us with her claws this passing ..."*

"Luck has claws?" asked Storm, "I don't even wanna know what you think of her."

"*Silence, fangless!*" One of them stepped forward, anger raging in her eyes.

"Well, that's my cue ..." Storm took a few cautious steps backward, careful not to fall from the branch. And then he started swearing. All was silent as the biggest one stalked towards him. With a great roar, it started charging, the other three following in pursuit. Storm could feel their sharp claws ripping through the stone ground as if it were clay.

Only a few seconds until they were upon him. One wrong move and the jaws of the closest Flare would be ripping his limbs apart. He clutched the branch tightly and took aim, glaring at the bobbing Einstein.

"Take this, you bastard!" Storm shouted. The branch whizzed through the air, a perfect throw. Einstein took off from the Kushala's head. As he did, one of the nowl's claws just barely scratched the tip of the Kushala's head. Storm grinned as the charging Kushala came to a dead stop, curled his powerful neck upwards and rested its flaring crimson eye on the pipe-smoking nowl. Einstein's eyes opened fully for the first time since Storm had seen him.

"Ha!" Storm cried. "Now you're going to get it!" The other Kushala had stopped as well, all of them staring at the nowl. Einstein was noticeably panicked, flapping his little wings faster than ever before and gaining height little by little.

"Yes!" Storm screamed. "Take him down! Eat him and ... WAIT, DON'T EAT THE SCARF!" All crimson eyes turned on him.

"Whoops, gotta go—!" He swore and laughed, turning and flashing back through the trees. He could feel the pounding of the earth behind him as the massive creatures tore down the forest in pursuit. They had found prey, and he was it. He could hear the ripping of tree trunks and the ferocious roars singing a premonition of his death. He could not fall. He could not stop. Only run. Fast. Faster.

"Some Kings of Neverend you are!" Storm taunted.

"Can't even catch me through the forest!" Storm flipped from tree to tree, than flashed forward a hundred feet, landing on the ground. With a single step, he flashed forward another hundred feet and landed on a branch thirty feet off the ground. Behind him he noticed only three of the four Kushalas tearing a path of destruction through the trees, saliva dripping from their fanged mouths and their blood red eyes locked on him.

Storm switched to the treetops. He had no idea where he was going. He was in an area of the forest he seldom visited; close to the northern edge, he guessed. A branch nearly smashed his face, cleanly cutting a slit in his cheek as he dodged it. How much longer could he run? More importantly, what about the trial? Now, he had no idea where Einstein was, or how he would catch him.

He had no idea what to do. Not that he really even had the time to figure it out as he was running for his life. Should he stop and fight the Kushala? No, that would be foolish—not even the old man could take on several full-grown Kushala.

"Shit!" he screamed. "What am I supposed to do!? Shit!!!"

He could hear the roars behind him, closing in. Trying to think of a plan, he slipped on a branch and fell through the trees, a hundred-foot drop to the ground. Pain assailed him as he slammed into branch after branch, and one crack to his side knocked the wind out of him. Gasping, he managed to catch a glance of the Kushala: they were still coming, gazing up at him as he fell towards them. Fear kicked in his instincts, and Storm's hand shot out, grasped a branch and under-flipped his body atop of it. With a deep breath he bolted in a new direction. The Kushalas' breath was hot on his back. A burst of light came before him as he passed a final tree.

His heart stopped along with his body. He had somehow run out onto one of the edges of Falia and began to slide to slow his run. His slide came to a stop with his toes hanging over the cliff; rocks and dirt fell to the empty sky beneath.

Storm swore again, "this is really not my day."

He could feel bloodlust overwhelming him. The three massive creatures skulked out of the shadows of the trees.

They ran their claws through the thick dirt, eyes only on him, and the putrid smell of their venomous tails seemed to overwhelm all the air in the clearing. Storm fought an urge to vomit. Covering his nose he took several breaths through his mouth.

"You guys seriously reek," he muttered.

"And you smell of fear and fresh meat ..." snickered one of the Flares.

Storm's hand slowly reached to his hilt. He didn't want to have to do this, but if was a battle to see who's stronger, he'd be happy to play with these rancid creatures a little while. His temper was becoming more and more dangerous, his thoughts flickering back and forth between Einstein, the Flares and possibly not even passing the first trial.

"Just my fucking luck," he spit.

"It seems we have found you, Black Rains ... there is a request for your head among the Kings of Neverend, as you have called us in your pointless fleeing."

One Kushala stepped forth, and Storm knew which one was talking to him. Its forearm wings were tinted with a dark purple glow. Poison dripped thickly from its tail.

"Now we have found you. The Master of the Forest will be pleased with this. We would have never expected you to be alone this far north. It is out of your territory, Black Rains. I wonder where your kin is, Silvers Fangless. Where is he? It seems that for once, you are not together ... he is not here to save you this time."

Storm's ego flared, "save me!?" he cried. He tried to laugh it off, but his anger quickly turned to rage. "I don't need any saving from anyone," he said sharply. "How about I rip out your hearts and prove that to you?"

"Rip out our hearts? Yes ... let's see that." The Kushala took one step closer. Then another.

"Gladly," said Storm, taking a step forward as well. His hand clenched hard over the hilt of his blade.

"Your brethren has insulted the Kushala for far too long, Black

Rains. It is time you paid for your wrongdoings, in blood. Many winters we have lived in the shame of our defeat to the Ghost of the Forest, Silvers Fangless and you. But no more, one by one we will find you … One by one we will bleed you … And one by one, we will kill you."

"You know," said Storm, "I'm really not having a good day at all. Terrible, actually. And on top of that, I seem to be losing more and more control of my anger these days. But if you wanna test me right now, if you want a fight," he drew his blade out. "Know that I won't hold back."

Storm fell silent as Einstein flew out of the treetops. He soared over the three Kushala and fluttered just over Storm's head until he was sitting safely in a tree away from the cliff. He left several puffed smoke rings in his wake.

Storm grinned. Well, one problem solved—now he wouldn't have to go through the trouble of finding his ridiculous pipe-smoking nowl.

He heard a vicious roar and the *crack* of a tree trunk snapping in half. The fourth Kushala, the biggest of them all, stalked out of the forest. Its limbs rippled with muscles, snapping the roots of trees as it walked. Stopping before the three, it roared thunderously, shaking the trees all around. Storm's arm tensed. Three was maybe possible—maybe. But four, and especially with this one as the fourth, was not looking good.

A strange light caught Storm's eye as the same airvras from the clearing floated out from the trees and came to a stop above the Kushalas. *Great. This stupid bubble, again.* The Announcer's voice was absolutely the last thing he wanted to hear while staring into the face of his quick approaching end.

"Ah! We found him at last!" the Announcer crowed. "And it seems that our flightless contestant has somehow managed to land himself in an even thicker predicament than before! These vicious Kushala—and ladies and gents, get a load of the big one, a real monster if I've ever seen one!—have him cornered against the edge of the cliffs. They are inching closer by the second and I can feel their ferocity and bloodlust in the air! If only he could fly, if only he wasn't the only contestant in the Soldier Games unable to break the barrier of earth and sky! What will he do!?"

"Shut the fu—" Storm roared.

One of the Kushala roared aggressively, causing the other three to back off. It didn't surprise him. This particular Flare had a fierce appearance, as if it had seen a lifetime of bloodshed. Its black scales were tainted with silver tips, and of the four it seemed the oldest, the most primeval. Storm's hand began to shake, his heartbeat thumping strongly in his chest. A sudden ancient voice broke his mind like the shattering of glass. With every possible strength, Storm resisted the urge to fall to his knees under its pressure.

"I can taste your fear, fangless. Yes, fangless. I will not name you as the others do, for your kind do not deserve names. I know not why my kind has been unable to kill you, but the stories of you and your kin have angered me for far too long. How I've longed to meet you … in all the ages of this timeless land, there has only ever been one to escape me. Yet, you are not he, although you will share the same fate he did. For he is already dead. That is the fate of those who defy us. You have nowhere to run. If you could fly, you would not be standing before us. A hatchling with a broken wing fearing only for its life has no place in Neverend. I will protect you from a cruel death by giving you a quick one. Oh, how I've longed for your blood, fangless! Remember my name, for I am Cerberith, descendent of Cerberus, the original God of our kind."

Storm grasped his trembling hand with his other. He could feel a fatigue coming over him, begging him to sleep. Everything was growing hazy, dim, and faint. He had heard of the Kushala having their own unique abilities. This was sure to be one of them. He knew not what it was, only that if he succumbed to it, he would surely die. Pulling his blade from his sheath, he ran the sharp edge along the top of his wrist, cutting himself deeply. The pain reawakened his senses—but the warm, fresh blood stirred the Kushala's bloodlust. The primeval beast Cerberith took to the air, its fangs slashing down towards him. One second. No, not even that. He could no longer hear or breathe, and stepped backwards only to find that there was nowhere to go. He fell. The sharp of the silver fang came an inch from his chest before falling away from him, as if a chain had wrapped around his body and was dragging him to safety.

No. Not to safety. The cliff rose quickly before his eyes. He was falling. The glare of the Kushala grew distant as he fell faster. The wind rushed violently. His senses returned.

Shit! I forgot about the cliff!!! The wind tore at his body as he picked up speed. He turned over, facing the empty sky. Storm again swore loudly, and began spinning. He tried to focus his aura but nothing seemed to be working.

"Calm down, calm down, calm down, calm down, *CALM DOWN, CALM DOWN!!!!*" Far, far above, one tiny speck floated in the sky. Einstein.

"Stupid bird!!!" he screamed to the heavens. Storm could practically visualize Einstein's slanted little eyes grinning at him. Anger became the sole ruler of his emotions. Rotating once again to face downward, he closed his eyes.

"I can do this! I have to do this! I've done this thousands of times in Inner Depths! What's the difference!? There's no damn difference! Why am I such a weak piece of shit!?" But all of his skills in flying and all of his experience were gone. No matter how hard he tried, it was futile. Why was it like this? Why couldn't he do it!? WHY!? He wanted to destroy his own body for lack of discipline and kill everything around him. Yet, nothing was around him. This thought pained him even more. He would die alone.

Anger overruled him in a way that had never happened before. He imagined killing Einstein happily, and in cold blood, dragging his crimson scarf from his neck. He imagined plucking his feathers one by one from his body before he died. Thoughts of his decrepit grandfather came before his eyes and he wished the old man had never saved him and Caim in the first place so long ago. It was the old man's fault after all that he was going to die. He felt his body hit the maximum falling speed. The wind was roaring. He thought of Caim, his stupid brother Caim. How he wished he could take a blade to his ... it was then the most wicked smile to ever appear on Storm's face showed itself. All of his fears seemed to be slipping away. All replaced by a much more powerful emotion, true hatred.

And so a foreign voice spoke to his mind, *"You fall needlessly ... Storm."*

Storm's eyes shot open. Looking around there was nothing, only sky. The voice was cold and cruel, daunting and ominous. It had left him with shivers running through every bone of his body. Yet, with his anger he could hardly feel fear anymore.

"I have been watching you for a long time, Storm ... From the shadows, ever since you were a child. Even now I watch you fall through the endless abyss. Do you wish to live, Storm? Of course you do ... but should you?" The voice was a whisper of death, and Storm could not discern if it was real or not. *"You are much too powerful to die here, Storm ... Or are you? Your brother has defeated you ... the pathetic bird has defeated you ... maybe you should die here. Maybe you do belong in a grave, Storm. We both know the weak have no place among the living."*

Storm's eyes flashed around as he tumbled through the sky.

"Who the hell are you!?" Storm screamed to the skies. Nothing answered him. His fists clenched harder than ever before, his nails biting into his flesh and springing forth streams of blood. His heart pounded in his chest like a violent drum and his muscles began to spasm erratically.

His clothing suddenly flashed from white to black, as if he were passing the boundaries of life and death. The falling had grown silent. The wind no longer ravaged him. Soria was growing distant. The clenching of his teeth was unbearable; in a moment they'd shatter.

"No ... I will not die here," answered Storm, speaking aloud to the voice. His fall had reached maximum velocity for a minute, and still there was nothing beneath him but dark emptiness. He hit a cloud and all was dark.

"That is the answer I wanted to hear, Storm ... Now, if you

want to live, I can help you. I can save you. My power will be your power. It is mine, and I shall give it to you."

"Who are you?" asked Storm.

"If you do not know, then I cannot tell you, Storm. But I do not wish you to die. I can lend you my power—I can lend you my –"

"NO!!!!" Storm screamed louder than he had ever screamed before, his voice cracking. He grasped his head and pulled his hair angrily. He wrenched his eyes open. Tears were streaming down his face and he couldn't tell if it was from falling or—

"I don't … need your help … I don't need ANYONE'S HELP!"

"But Storm –"

"I SAID I DON'T NEED YOUR GODDAMN HELP!!!"

"Then die like the weak animal you are."

Storm's eyes snapped open. "Get the fuck out of my head or I'll kill you … I swear to the gods I'll rip you apart piece by piece. I'll kill you, I swear –" And something cracked in Storm. Something deep within him. Something locked away in the very core of his being.

Something was crawling over him. Growing from him. No, maybe he was growing from something. A change was occurring, and he knew not what it meant. He had been falling at a speed he couldn't even run, yet he was slowing. Storm eventually came to a stop, lying horizontally in the empty sky; his arms and legs hung limp from his sides. As his body turned slowly upright, he opened his eyes. Something was strange. He could feel something … different about himself. All his senses were clearer, much clearer. He could hear a faint buzzing. Something brushed his leg. Gazing down slowly, his eyes fell on a long black tail lined with midnight shards. He grabbed it, feeling pain, and let go. He watched his tail wrap around his waist. Or felt it rather.

A tail?! He had a tail? Everything slowed down. Everything around him was pristine. Falia sat high above him. The lands of Falia. The bottom of a floating land was all he could see. He felt something behind him.

He looked over his shoulders and his eyes opened wide. Stretching from his shoulders were two blazing wings of crimson aura. They were powerful and sharp, crackling with a buzzing energy. He gazed at his hands; his wrists were layered in a thicker version of his normal Hollow armor. It was sharper, stronger and had a different feel to its aura than usual. Why was everything about himself similar but different?

XLVIII – A SHIMMER OF EMERALD AND CRIMSON

A phenomenal energy surged through him; he had no doubt he'd become something much more powerful than he had ever been. Everything he had once thought to be strong was dimmed. Caim was pathetic. The old man was nothing. His arms flexed powerfully. Every muscle in his body was bigger, stronger. Even his cage of aura was five, no, ten times the capacity it had once been. Everything was ... he was ...

Storm blinked, and all was gone. The tail was gone. The wings were gone. Everything had vanished, yet he remained floating in the sky. The power was no longer with him. He was normal again. Unknowingly, a wake of crimson energy lifted from his body like a veil. There was no voice. He clenched his hands over and over wondering what had happened. He felt as if he had just awoken in a dream. Fear was no more. Hatred lingered but a sense of calm was left the ruler of his body. A fatigue as if he hadn't slept in days came over him. He wished to fall, but couldn't. His eyes looked up and found a single speck, floating high above him.

"Einstein ..." he muttered. Every muscle in his body tensed. Silence was all he wished for. Silence and revenge. "You better fly fast, bird ... because I just overcame my fear of flying."

Cracking his knuckles, he shot up into the sky like an arrow.

Einstein shuddered as he felt a chill creep through his body. Glancing his slanted eyes downward, he felt his heart drop. A black and seething flame of aura was all he could see rising from the depths, as if Mortal Aeryx had fired an arrow of fire upon Soria. The fire was powerful and full of bloodlust, almost as if the persona of the Kushala had been warped and transferred. A ravenous beast was coming fast, and Einstein could feel it.

Storm watched as Einstein took off flying. This time he could tell the nowl was serious as he picked up speed, beating his wings rapidly. Storm looked ahead of where Einstein was flying and noticed the Enhancement Ring in the sky. An idea came to him. Everything seemed to be moving slower. He was exhausted, confused, but calmer than before. He couldn't grasp what had just happened. It was unlike any other physical, mental or spiritual experience he had ever encountered.

Still, Storm screamed past the cliff, past the Kushala who were glaring evilly at him.

Revenge, was his only thought.

Turning in midair, Storm ripped his katana from its sheath and focused his aura; a black flame rippled along his blade. Slashing the air, a seething wave of deathly aura fired from his blade's edge like a crescent arc of black energy. He grinned evilly as the devastating attack struck the side of the cliff a smaller Flare was standing on. He saw the cliff shatter beneath it, and watched in glee as it struggled for balance. It was too late. The Flare fell howling from the cliff's edge.

Storm laughed wickedly, "Whooo!!!! Now I feel better!"

Storm sheathed his blade and flew toward the smoke ring. How did he overcome his fear of death? How was he flying? He didn't know. Only that the nowl was in his grasp. Questions could be answered later. Storm passed through the ring, closing the distance rapidly. The winged key pulsed against his chest. A grin curved across his face as he grasped the key.

Click!

Storm came to a dead stop. His black aura vanished. Everything was heavy.

"What the ... can I not catch a break today!?" he screamed desperately, trying to keep himself afloat. Storm struggled to move towards Einstein, who had stopped and turned his eyes back to him.

"NO!" he screamed. "I will not lose like this! No!!" Storm whipped his body back and forth as if trying to break invisible chains. He could barely move his arms and felt himself starting to sink downwards. Einstein floated down towards Storm, flying in little circles around his head while puffing away on his pipe, taunting him with slanted eyes.

"You damned bird!" yelled Storm. "You think you're so damn clever, don't you!?"

A grin curved across his face as he made *clicking* sounds from his mouth. The winged key was resting against his chest, glowing.

"Got you," he whispered. Einstein's eyes widened as Storm vanished. A split second later Storm was floating inches past Einstein's shoulder. The nowl froze. Storm placed his hand on Einstein's shoulder.

"Now, what to do with you ..." Storm's fingers closed over the scarf and ripped it from the nowl's neck. "Looks like you misjudged me," he said. "Good thing about the announcer is that *everyone* can hear him. Landfill was the effect that plagued my stupid brother earlier, wasn't it?" He cocked his eyes. Einstein fluttered away, his entire body trembling. Storm's hand found its way to his hilt. He grasped the hilt of his blade, turning the blade to the creature's neck. His eyes were not just wicked, his whole face was evil and laughing.

"Just ... kidding."

He laughed maniacally, and let the silver blade slide back into its sheath. With a quick turn, the nowl bolted in the opposite direction, fleeing for his life.

Storm heard a loud outburst of cheering erupt through Soria. He raised the scarf high above his head. The announcer descended from above and spoke. "Look at this, ladies and gents! I can hardly believe my eyes! The contestant has done it! Einstein has been caught, I repeat, EINSTEIN HAS BEEN CAUGHT!

"And what a way to win! Pretending to have taken on the status effect of Landfill, he used Einstein's ego against him! What a great kickoff to this cycle's Soldier Games! I can tell it's going to be incredible this cycle!!!"

Storm glared up at the announcer. A second later, he gazed back at the distant speck that was the Arena of Kings and burst through the air toward the finish line. A thousand thoughts were racing through his mind. Why did he feel like this? What was this anger that had been born in him? Who had been speaking to him? What had happened to him beneath Falia? Had the crimson wings of aura and the black tail been real? He couldn't tell … the only thing he knew was that if they were, he had definitely come upon the next level of strength.

The words of the old man echoed in his mind, *"One day … you will glimpse the wings."*

XLIX – A Change in the Winds

Back within the White Castle, at the top of the Spearway to Eden; past a grove of silver-barked trees and up upon a white balcony stood the Empress and her four guardians. The Empress stood gracefully upon the tip of the carved balcony with her hands on the railing and her eyes locked on the airvras. She gazed at the image of a swordsman with black hair and emerald eyes.

"Wouldja looka dat?" beamed Lord Falkor. "Truly unexpec'ed!"

"Indeed," Lady Scylla said. "There is something *special* about the contestants this cycle. A strange energy lingers over the lands of Soria today."

Lord Falkor raised an eyebrow yet said nothing.

The Empress turned around. "Sakura, it seems you aren't the only one who has caught Einstein now!" The Empress winked at Sakura and whispered, "But you're still our favorite."

Sakura lowered her head. "I am not worthy of your praise, my Empress."

It was true Sakura had been the only other in history to catch Einstein, but something else had been bothering her. It was moments before the nowl was captured when she had felt it. A power darker than she had felt in many cycles with the exception of Grahf. It was dark and ravenous, full of bloodlust and hatred, as if a specter had slid his scythe past her throat. It left her breathing heavy and her in a cold sweat. She wondered what Lady Scylla thought of the dark power. Looking at her, her face left no impression to how she felt.

Could it be possible that such a contestant could exist in this Soldier Games? Why hadn't she heard of such a recruit? His or her power would have been sure to impress both the Force and the Shield. She shivered. It wasn't a normal power. Something was evil about it. An ominous feeling sat on her shoulders as she contemplated everything she could not understand. Had it been the black swordsman who caught Einstein? He certainly didn't look that powerful...and she could feel his energy now and it was nothing, less than even the weakest of the Force or the Shield. She turned and looked at Vasuki. An intrigued grin was curved across his face. Why was he so happy? She concealed her confusion.

- - - -

Standing outside the Alchemy shop in Trestles, the old woman who had once tried to trick Storm watched one of the airvras. A line of shops had placed CLOSED signs on their windows, and many of their owners were sitting on chairs outside, gazing up at the couple of airvras projecting the first trial. The wind was blowing sharp and cold. Soria was erupting in cheer.

Storm's figure came unto the airvras; he was holding the grandfather clock scarf. The old woman gazed into his eyes as she puffed away on a silver pipe. Somehow, the swordsman boy had snuck his way into the Soldier Games and successfully caught Einstein. The airvras flashed closer to Storm's face. She watched his eyes shimmer from emerald to crimson.

"Now that's something I haven't seen in many long cycles," she muttered. "Your eyes, boy, are of a darker and different swordsman than the one I once met. What's happening to you out there?"

An old man with a long scarf and shaggy brown hair reached over and touched her shoulder. "Can you believe that, Graelsi? The boy caught Einstein! I thought he was dead in that fall! And there were even four Flares chasing him!" He sighed. "It's hard for me to even believe the Flares still exist … haven't seen or heard of one in so long."

The old woman took a long puff of her pipe. "They will always exist," she said. "Among many other things that we wish didn't." Graelsi closed her eyes.

After a moment Graelsi stood, grabbed a green sweater and pulled it over her shoulders. "I'm going to the Arena of Kings," she said. "I'm going to see the end of this Soldier Games."

The old man stared up at her. "Well now, this isn't like you at all …"

"Times are changing," she said.

The old man smiled, "Times are always changing. By the way, you didn't happen to borrow some white paint from the front of my store last night, did you?"

Graelsi looked up at the airvras. Storm was floating in the sky holding Einstein's scarf. The hollow on his wrists was white. With a grin she kept walking. "Sorry old friend, but I can't say I did. But knowing you, I'd say it's probably somewhere right in front of your eyes."

- - - -

Still watching from the shadows of District Four, Lucius, Rei and Dewey gazed at the airvras floating in the center of the white courtyard. Hundreds of Falians stood around them cheering loudly. The kids were cheering and running through the crowd. The willows were singing. The bells were ringing, and the smell of food was everywhere. Storm was holding the scarf in his hand.

Dewey stared in awe at the airvras. He blinked, then looked over at Lucius.

"You have got to be kidding me!" Lucius said, nearly dropping a clay cup of water.

"He did it," whispered Rei. "HE DID IT!!" She grabbed Lucius's hand and he dropped the clay cup. It shattered on the ground.

"Whoa!" cried Lucius, raising his hands. Dewey cracked a smile.

"Sorry," said Rei with an awkward smile.

"That's a bad omen," said Lucius. He looked down at the broken cup with apprehension.

"I don't care," cried Rei. "He won. He can do it!"

Dewey took a step forward and with it, a deep breath. "Whether he can do it or not isn't really the question," he began. "When you two first started trying to tell me that those two kids from way back had returned from Neverend I was skeptical, but this … this is just a whole different level of insanity. I mean, every part of my being is telling me not to believe you. From the tryouts to the nobles in Melri's … from stealing the armor to actually sneaking into the Soldier Games. The Soldier Games!" He clasped his hands behind his head and looked hard at Storm, "But it's definitely him. I remember that face, that glint in his eyes. If they grew up in Neverend then we already know they're tougher than most grown men."

"And?" Lucius said, looking quite taken back. He slowed his speech. "They. Broke. Into. The. Soldier. Games." He played out each word with a gesture of his hands. "Doesn't matter if they are tougher than a grown man. Are we forgetting what they are doing? They are either going to be killed in the games, or executed afterward for being found out." Dewey crossed his arms and didn't say anything. His eyes had a solemn look to them.

"Why are you so negative?" Rei snapped.

"Why!?? Cried Lucius. "Forget Caim, but now Storm has to enter Falling Tower! Did you forget that? Did you forget that the games just become more and more dangerous with each round? He got lucky Rei, and honestly, I don't even think it can be called luck at this point. If he would have just lost, then he might have survived in the end. But now ..." his voice trailed off.

Rei's smile faded. "Why are you being like this? They have nobody. Nobody knows what they are doing. They are alone, fighting with no support. The least you can do is give them your belief!"

Dewey gave Rei an appreciative look and smiled, "I will give them my support." Rei looked at Dewey and then laid her hand on his arm, "Thank you, Dewey." His cheeks burned red.

Rei turned back to the screen. She wondered if she was doing the right thing. Was believing in them the only thing she could do? Or had she really encouraged Storm to go to his death? And what about his brother? The airvras switched to a boy with silver hair and awkward-looking armor. She couldn't help but laugh at the sight. Caim looked ridiculous peeling off his silver armor. Her eyes widened.

"Caim," she said. "He still hasn't—"

"Forget about him," Lucius spit. "He got Bolt. He already lost."

L - Caim Versus Bolt

aim struggled heavily as he inched his way toward the smoky ring. The fifty-fold weight increase of Landfill was slowly killing him and he knew it. No matter how hard he fought it, he could feel himself draining. He could feel his aura pouring out of his body like sand through an hourglass. All around him Bolt flew in circles, stopping every now and then to tap him on the head with his wing, squawking at him and doing everything possible to taunt him.

"Oh … you just—keep that up. I'll get you," Caim spit out as he pushed on. A few times he'd tried to grab the scarf but wasn't nearly quick enough. He felt as if mountains were attached to his arms. His breathing had become incredibly heavy and the thought that he would soon plummet to his death crawled into the back of his mind. Minute after painful minute he pushed forward, inching along. Everything soon grew quiet. Fatigue and pain were all that remained. Consciousness came to and fro. He looked up hazily at the ring before him. Just a few more seconds and he'd pass through. Shards of glass were twisting racing around his lungs like a tornado. The winged key pulsed from his chest. Barely

163

finding the strength to grasp it, he clicked the key together and passed through the ring.

Click!

Caim felt lightness consume him as he shot high into the sky. A torrential downpour of aura raced through his every muscle, limb and fingertip. Energy exploded from him as he felt his cage of aura replenishing at an absurd rate.

"Whoa!" he yelled. "I'm me again! I'm so light!" He flashed around in a circle. "Wait, what's happening ..." Aura seeped out of his body in every direction, as if it were dripping off of him.

"I feel ... amazing!" Stretching his arms up to the sky, he found Bolt and pointed at him. "See that, bird? I made it past the stupid snakes! Now I'm coming to get you!"

He could hear the crackling of his energy as he flexed his arms. He felt as strong as he'd ever been. A hundred meters ahead of him was the nowl, spread horizontally in the air with his wing laid over his face.

"Quit screwing with me!" yelled Caim, and flashed forward. In an instant Bolt shot upwards, surprised at Caim's sudden burst of speed. Caim felt that the nowl's speed was something truly unrivaled in the world of flying. Despite the massive surge of aura the winged key had given him, he still couldn't move at the same speed as Bolt. It was as if the nowl had some connection with the sky, a bond that made the two, one. Caim flashed forward as he felt his aura pouring out in bright flames. He soared through the air, arms tucked to his sides, piercing through the clouds like an arrow.

Bolt took a sudden turn upwards. Caim followed. Passing through a cloud, he saw Bolt dodge past one of the Shepherds. A huge burst of wind nearly knocked its rider off as Bolt flew by. A second burst of wind shook the rider as Caim shot by a split second later. Bolt took a hard dive, and aimed back towards Falia. Caim hadn't realized how high they had traveled. Falia looked distant, the forest of Neverend was a blanket of emerald, and for once, he could see the top of the great tree Nocturnis Aqua. Its tip seemed to shimmer with gold and silver, as if an ancient kingdom were kept secret at its top. Senyria glistened at its base; four strings of silver stretched out from it. Caim noticed Bolt tuck his wings to his body, going into a full speed dive. Caim tucked his head and dove straight after him.

Cloud after cloud. Faster and faster. The wind slashed his face and thundered in his ears; he could barely see anything. Bolt was moving so fast Caim wondered if Falia would move a little bit if the nowl were to strike it at full speed—he'd probably just pass through it like an indestructible arrow. He imagined everyone on Falia stumbling upon Bolt's impact. He grinned stupidly. Would Falia even budge?

Storm would think that's a stupid question... .

Caim's eyes focused back in on Bolt. The nowl was not slowing down. Falia was rising up toward them, growing bigger and bigger. Caim didn't slow down either. Neverend grew bigger and bigger. In the corner of one of his eyes, he saw one of the silver rivers reach a distant cliff. The river was hurtling itself off of the cliff, pouring into the sky as a waterfall of glistening silver.

A Skyfall!!!

His attention snapped back to Bolt. Falia was upon them. They were at the height of the tallest trees. Bolt was heading straight towards the cliff. He was going to crash into the cliff! Caim braced himself for Bolt's impact.

The steep, rocky cliffs came before Bolt and he vanished before Caim's eyes.

"He ... vanished?" The wind was screaming in his face. He didn't know where to go. Anxiety rocketed through his heart. He was going to crash. A random opening in the cliff revealed itself to him. A cave? Without thinking, he flew full speed into the dark hole. Dozens of hanging vines slapped his face violently as he passed through. Slashing them away with his hands, he tried to maintain his balance. He swerved to the side, missing a sharp stalactite by inches. He couldn't see anything. Everything was pitch black.

After a few seconds of flying in complete darkness, his eyes adjusted. He came to a floating stop, his eyes taking in the sight of a dark cave, lined with thousands of hanging stalactites. The walls were steep and the air was murky. He could feel wetness on his fingertips.

"Stupid bird ... where'd you go?"

Peering forward he saw him. There, a hundred feet ahead was Bolt, dashing in between the dozens of stone icicles. At the very end of the cave was a faint light, a tiny broken circle in the darkness.

This is so cool!! Thought Caim. *How did Storm and I never know about this!? We'll come back here and adventure once we've won the tournament!*

Ahead, Bolt moved like a perfect blur. Not only was he beyond fast, he had perfect form and flew between the spiked rock icicles with complete ease. Barrel-rolling through some of them, he spun and dived and dashed towards the end of the cave. Caim shot forward trying to follow Bolt's path, but he was flying much faster than he was used to in a tight space, and before long he realized he couldn't move as well as Bolt in the treacherous cavern.

A sharp hanging of stalactite came before him. It was too late to dodge. Caim crashed hard and fell to the ground, smashing through dozens of rocky stalagmites. He felt the sharp rock slice through his arms and hands as he came to a skidding stop. His clothing was soaked. Grasping his breastplate he ripped it off, then the helmet, followed by the greaves. Only the bracers remained. *Stupid armor,* he thought. *Makes me too damn slow. As long as my Hollow is painted white, I should be fine.* Caim jumped back to his feet and took off flying again, his white vest feathering out behind him. He soon smashed straight into another hanging spike and fell hard to the ground. He slid nearly thirty feet before finally stopping.

This wasn't working. He spit out blood. His hand flicked to the hilt of his Fallblade. If he couldn't dodge them, he might as well go through them. Caim focused his aura until it was flaming once again, and took up the pursuit of Bolt once more. The nowl was so fast that he could barely see him. He was nearing the distant light. The end of the cave. And then he stopped, turned and taunted Caim.

Fire came unto Caim's eyes. "Oh now you're going to get it!" he screamed. "Think you can just taunt me endlessly when you know this cave and I don't! Well, hah! Just wait, stupid bird! I will catch you!!"

Caim flew like a ball of white fire. Upon nearing the first chunk of hanging rock, he clicked out his Fallblade. He could hear the sliding of metal as he forced it out of its sheath and brought it down vertically through the rock. The rock split perfectly in two, and it seemed as if he were in slow motion as his face passed straight through the split halves. His speed instantly returned as he sped through the cave, even faster than before, slicing and dicing all that blocked his path. Pure destruction was left in his wake.

Caim's eyes narrowed on the end of the cave. It wasn't much farther. He watched Bolt turn and take off flying.

Soon enough, Caim burst out into the light and the open sky came before him. Coming to a skidding stop in the air, he looked up to find Bolt flying back towards Risia. He was flying just along the cliffs a little further ahead; a black dart against a rocky background. Caim sheathed his blade and continued his pursuit.

"You haven't lost me yet, bird!" he shouted angrily.

The voice of the announcer crackled to life above him. "Look at this, ladies and gents! I can hardly believe my eyes! The contestant has done it! Einstein has been caught, I repeat, EINSTEIN HAS BEEN CAUGHT!" Caim looked up, and realized that where he had come out of the cave was right beneath where Storm was floating in the sky. He was holding the scarf of his nowl.

Yosha! Storm caught his bird! His eyes focused back on Bolt. "Now it's my turn!!!" Caim increased his speed and soared through the next smoky ring Bolt had passed moments before. He felt the pulse of the key once again. It was a foreign pulse of power that made his whole body twitch.

"Please don't be the stupid weight one again!" He reached down and grabbed the key within his hands. Folding his fingers around the wings he *clicked* them together.

Click!

Caim stared in awe as a red beam of light shot forth from

the key—faster than he had ever seen anything move. It connected to Bolt's back a second later. A great force tugged on his chest, pulling him towards Bolt. Looking at the key, a strange silver ring of energy was floating around it. Before he could think, he felt his body hurtling forward as if he were being dragged by some mysterious and unrelenting force.

"WAHOO!!!!" screamed Caim as he was propelled through the air. He watched in pure delight as Bolt came closer, despite his attempts to fly faster. The distance between them steadily closed. They rose past the cliffs. Caim's eyes widened. Bolt was coming within range. The black scarf with the lightning bolt upon it was all Caim could see.

"Now ... YOU'RE MINE!!!!" Caim reached towards Bolt's back, the scarf only feet away.

"SORIA!" roared the announcer. All around both worlds, each and every airvras was focused on Caim's pursuit of Bolt. "It seems our contestant, cursed for being paired with Bolt, has finally come across good fortune! With the passing of the second Enhancement Ring his aura was completely replenished!! And now, upon passing the third Ring, it seems he has activated Magnetic Pull!!"

A wide grin curved across Caim's face. If he and Bolt were magnets drawn together, speed no longer mattered. Bolt was desperately doing everything in his power to avoid Caim's grasping hand. Barreling to the side, diving down and then up, Caim could only be pulled along for the ride.

The announcer's voice grew ecstatic. "No matter how hard Bolt tries I don't think he'll be able to escape this one! Could this be it!? Could this be the moment we've all been waiting for!? Could this really be the day Bolt is caught!?" His voice tone suddenly changed, "Wait ... what's this? It seems another contestant is flying straight at Bolt's pursuer!! What are those around her head!? Oh no, this isn't good. This isn't good at all! She's been charmed!!!"

Caim watched in shock as a young girl wearing dark leather armor and black gloves came out of nowhere. His eyes narrowed; little pink hearts were floating around her head as she charged straight at him.

"Wait … wait, wait, wait!!!" cried Caim, trying with all his energy to avert his path, but to no avail, he could not stop the pull. The girl reeled back her leather-gloved fist as she descended upon Caim, a ravenous look in her disdainful eyes.

"I'll be taking that scarf now!!" she yelled at Caim.

Caim's eyes looked blank. "Wait … I'm not a bird!!!" he screamed. She was inches away. He could not dodge. Caim felt her fist connect to his face. Hard. He felt like he had just been struck in the cheek by a sledgehammer. Blood trickled into his mouth as the momentum from being pulled doubled the impact of the girl's punch.

"ARE YOU CRAZY!?" Caim screamed as he catapulted past her, still being pulled by Bolt. Caim's hand shot to his Fallblade.

She turned and clenched her leather-gloved fist. "I won't let you get away!" she screamed before flying after him.

"I can't believe my eyes!" yelled the announcer. "It seems that one of our contestants has been charmed into believing that this contestant is in fact, her nowl!! Now she is charging relentlessly after this poor contestant who can't do much but hold on for dear life! I can't see where this is going but it isn't looking good. My, what a turn of luck for Bolt!! It looks like they're nearing the halfway point of the race now, and should be flying directly over the Bridge of Hierarchy!! For all of you watching near the bridge, turn your eyes to the sky! This is something you won't want to miss!"

Caim could feel his entire body being pulled faster than he could fly and there was nothing he could do about it. The enhancement was turning out to be more negative than positive, as he couldn't control the movement of where he wanted to go at all. He could see the towering shape of the coliseum coming clearly into view. The long black bridge streaming across the sky came before him. Turning to the side, he saw the tall silver tower in the center of Trestles surrounded by the massive white wall that caged the city.

Bolt started flying upward, passing through several clouds. They passed Trestles in a matter of seconds. The black bridge was directly to his left, the coliseum looming mightily in the distance. He focused back on the girl. She was fast, and gaining.

He considered the girl's path toward him, bracing for her next attack. Just then, he felt his stomach jump into his chest as he was sucked downwards. Lurching his head back around to Bolt, he realized that he was being pulled straight down towards the bridge.

"AHHH!!!" Caim screamed. Bolt was flying directly at the bridge. They'd both hit it at top speed.

Several Sorians watched over the edge of the bridge as Bolt zoomed past them as a black unstoppable blur; the wind from his speed sending a couple falling onto their backs and ripping the tops of several tents clean off.

"MOVE OUT OF THE WAY!!" screamed Caim just before he collided with the side of the bridge. An instant later he felt himself scraping down the side of it, tumbling over and over. Pain screamed through his body and it felt like he had been broken in half. Trying not to lose consciousness, he felt himself ripped down the side of the bridge before finally being freed from underneath it. He watched as Bolt soared before him—he must have shot upwards at the last possible second. Squinting his eyes hazily, Caim could see the pack of nowls up ahead. They had caught up.

Caim gasped, reaching for his ribs. At least one had been broken. He shook off the pain. It didn't matter. Nothing mattered. Only catching the scarf. Caim pushed himself faster towards Bolt, using the magnetic pull to his advantage.

"YOU WILL NEVER ESCAPE ME!" screamed a voice he wished he hadn't heard. The same heart-struck girl, disoriented by the effects of the enhancement ring's Charm, was coming down fast from above. Caim barely looked up in time to dodge her second punch, watching as she hurtled past him like a bullet. He watched her come to a skidding stop in the air, turn, and take off after him again. For a split second, he thought he noticed the number of pink hearts around her head dwindling in number.

Caim closed his eyes and focused. Despite all the pain in his body, he was going to do it. Despite the cracking of his ribs, the searing pain, the flashes of white and red in his mind, he would not give up. Pushing forward, he pulled desperately at his cage of inner aura. Wishing he could just release all of it with one burst, he swore loudly. Within moments, Bolt's speed had brought them upon the pack of contestants chasing their nowls. They had long since passed the coliseum and were now flying over Risia. The White Castle stood like a fairy tale in the distance, watching them. Caim dodged to the left, barely avoiding a contestant with a long black cloak and ornate bow on his back. Weaving in and out of nowls and contestants alike, Bolt passed through with unmatched haste.

Where was the next smoky ring!? He needed to break this chain or he'd never catch Bolt.

Caim struggled to focus as he took in the sight of contestants all around. Some had massive aura levels, and their energy flamed off of them brightly as they blasted forward in their individual pursuits. He could tell they were fatigued, and there were only about thirty of them still flying. He watched in horror as one contestant with bright red hair suddenly grasped his own neck; all the veins in his body were turning dark purple and bulging through his fair skin. A second later he fell from the sky.

"Oi! What are you doing!? You're going to die!!" screamed Caim.

Without hesitation Caim dropped, almost unable to move from the effects of the Magnetic Pull, and barely grasping the fallen contestant by the armor on his back, he launched the contestant towards Risia. He watched the contestant's body fly over the cliffs and smash into a wall before slowly sliding down it.

"Sorry!" yelled Caim. "That's gotta hurt! But at least you won't die!" He felt the pull drag him upwards, his eyes spinning around the dozens of nowls and contestants alike. Some of the others around him had dark black clouds covering their heads, and he could tell they had no idea where they were going. Some collided with one another, while others had strange timers over their heads. One girl with dark skin had a timer above her head with skulls floating around the dwindling numbers. Her face was overcome with terror. She came to a sudden stop, ripped the key from her neck and crushed it to dust. The timer vanished and she was disqualified. Her eyes were full of fear and her face a pallid, cold white.

Glancing to the side, his eyes found Ladon; his energy burning bright gold as he shot through the sky, twisting and turning. Their eyes met for a split second before Ladon descended upon his own nowl. Caim watched Ladon flash and appear directly in front of the all-white nowl wearing a red scarf. The nowl had nowhere to go and crashed straight into Ladon. They tumbled through the sky before separating. Wearily, Ladon held his hand up in the air, holding the red scarf in his hand.

"I DID IT!!!" he cried. "GET HIM, GEOERGE!!!" he screamed as Caim whizzed by.

Out of the corner of his eye, he watched as a big black nowl dropped away from the flock. Its back had a strange lump on it and around its neck was a bright blue scarf. He tried to focus as he saw the nowl fly out and over Risia, completely off course, fading off into the distance. Where was that one going?

Far past where the mysterious nowl had descended, and far past the White Castle was a great black tower. It was tall and terrible and daunting; an energy unlike anything he had ever felt emanated from it, and it reminded him of the dead. A shiver ran through his body. Between the tower and the White Castle was a similar looking forest to Neverend. He glanced back to the tower. Around its tip was an enormous crimson ribbon that waved strongly in the wind. The ribbon must have been hundreds of feet long and fifty feet wide. It was something he had never seen before. A black tower on the farthest tip of Risia. It was something he could have never seen from Falia. He soon realized they were nearing the end of Risia, and that Soria was not as big as he thought it was when he was a kid.

Turning back to Bolt, he saw another Enhancement Ring coming upon them.

"Finally!" This time it was different, though. It was sitting horizontally, instead of standing upright in the air. He would have to dive down to go through it. Looking past it, the path looked as if it were leading down under Risia. Upon passing through the ring, he would be flying down past the cliffs. Several others were passing through it as he thought. *Why is the path taking us downwards? Shouldn't we be going around Risia?*

The words of the announcer broke his concentration. "I cannot believe my eyes! They are moving so fast the airvras can barely keep up! It seems our contestants are reaching the final Enhancement Ring. The beginning of the end it is called, the crux of the course! They will soon descend beneath the land of Risia, where they will have to deal with something much worse than anything they've encountered before. Sixteen contestants have grasped their scarves and fourteen have returned to the bridge! This is it! The end is near! Everyone, keep your eyes peeled at the bridge, for that is where the true victors will rise!!!"

Bolt dashed in front of another Shepherd, only to have the black-winged Sleipnir flash its teeth at him. Dodging just barely to the side, Caim avoided impact and felt his body twist downwards and through the final ring. Upon passing, he felt the pulse of the winged key. Just as he grasped it, he felt a great force strike the back of his head, blurring his vision.

"YOU AGAIN!?" screamed Caim wearily, looking up at the young girl raising her fist. They were both falling fast, way past the edge of Risia. The sharp cliffs rose speedily at his sides. Angrily, he looked at the girl chasing him. His eyes gazed to her chest where her glowing winged key came before his eyes. An idea came upon him.

Caim braced himself for impact. Slowing his descent, he

felt her come upon him, her fist inching close to his face. Dodging just slightly, he avoided her punch while reaching forward and grabbing her key.

Click!

In that instant, the circling pink hearts faded from her head. Still falling and twisting with their faces nearly touching, she came to. She looked awkwardly at Caim, then peered down to his hand, which was resting on her chest.

"You pervert!" she yelled, swinging at him. Caim pushed himself off of her and turned to face Bolt. He grabbed his own key. "I don't care what I get! I will catch you!" And he clicked the two wings together one last time.

Click!

…

Thump—Thump

Caim could feel his heart beat slow as everything around him became silent. Even the whistling of the high-speed fall faded to nothing. And then, just as the silence was engulfing him, he could hear everything. He could hear the breathing of the young girl still floating high above him. He could tell she was confused about what had happened. He could hear the flapping of Bolt's wings in the distance, steady and in perfect unison, gaining distance. He could hear the cheering of everyone on Soria. The pounding of their feet. He could see nearly twice as far as normal and with perfect clarity. He could feel *everything*. The spirit of the land, the contestants, the nowls. Their beating hearts and their life forces, even their emotions. It was as if pure instinct had taken over.

"Now, this … this, I can work with this." Caim turned back around and faced the downward fall.

He felt the Magnetic Pull snap between Bolt and his descent slowed. He was floating directly beneath the bottom tip of Risia, and he could see thousands of dangling green vines. He was underneath Risia. It looked like a forest flipped upside down. He watched as Bolt weaved in and out of the hanging vines; massive leaves filled with water hung from some of their sides. But most of all, he felt something strange about the underside of Risia. A powerful current of energy awaited him like a violent and raging ocean. A sliver of fear slid through his body and he took a deep breath. Something about being under Risia was dangerous.

High above he heard the faint voice of the announcer. "As I'm sure you all know, Soria is surrounded by a huge magnetic field that clashes with the magnetic field that hovers over Mortal Aeryx. Imagine Soria as being surrounded by an enormous bubble of aura. Then imagine Mortal Aeryx as also being wrapped in a similar bubble. These two bubbles sit atop one another and their currents do not allow one or the other to pass. This is the theory of great Lord Galileo for why our lands stay afloat in the sky."

The announcer took a breath as Caim scanned the dangerous path. "However, the most dangerous thing about this is the gravity beneath Risia. It is thrown into complete chaos down there because of this bubble and the energy it creates. Now stay with me, if you aren't careful, and I mean *very* careful, you can be sucked down and forced between the two bubbles. What a tragedy that would be … for in between the two bubbles lies the Calm Zone—an area that separates Soria and Mortal Aeryx. If you are forced into it … there is no return. It is a place with no energy. A place with the current of Mortal Aeryx pushing up from below and the current of Risia pushing down from above. No contestant who has ever fallen into the Calm Zone … has ever returned."

Caim closed his eyes and he could feel them. The converging points of the two bubbles seemed to suck everything close to them inwards, to their cores. Yet, he could not feel the Calm Zone. Just a tempest of clashing energy all around.

Without hesitation, Caim's eyes opened and he flashed under the floating land. Instantly, he could feel a sudden weight whipping his body all around. It was unlike anything he could have expected. Several of the contestants were falling out through the vines; the hectic energy had taken their consciousness. There was nothing he could do. Even at the speed he flew, he couldn't stop it. He started smacking into the long and thick vines, each one slowing him considerably.

High above, one of the contestants was climbing along the base of Risia. A giant chunk of earth broke where he was climbing; the contestant dashed forward, barely making it to safety. The rock fell. Caim could barely turn in time to see what was happening before the massive rock smashed into his body. His reflexes were completely broken. The pain consumed him. Everything was dark. He could feel himself falling, but he couldn't move. The more he struggled the more he was forced down, and soon he could feel the tempest energy ripping through his every limb; forcing him to succumb to its god-like power.

He felt himself pass through what felt like a barrier of power and glass; shreds of aura tore through his arms, ripping through the bone armor on his shoulders. Blood sprayed into the torrent and whipped around him splashing his face. And then all energy was gone. He came to a stop.

"Did I stop myself?" he said under his breath.

No, he hadn't.

He was completely still.

Floating in an area completely calm.

- - - -

Back on the bridge, near where the race had begun, Storm leaned silently against a wall, his victory scarf hanging from his back pocket. Sixteen other contestants with scarves were around him, all quiet. Many of them had lost friends. Suddenly, Storm's eyes opened wide. He could not feel his brother's aura anywhere. It had vanished. Completely gone. Then without moving a muscle, Storm closed his eyes once again.

Sorry brother, it seems this is where we part. Only the truly strong survive in this world.

LI – The Final 18

Ronin opened his eyes and turned his gaze toward Soria.

"You've sensed it," whispered Lady Vale. She turned her eyes in the same direction.

"Caim has fallen to the Calm Zone. I fear he will never return. Will you abandon what only you can do and save him, or will you leave him to die?"

Ronin's eyes closed slowly.

- - - -

Rei and Lucius watched in horror as the announcer spoke. "Everyone, I am truly saddened to announce that the contestant chasing Bolt has fallen through the barrier and now lies somewhere in the Calm Zone. We know not how he fell, but his presence has completely vanished. Bolt is … once again, victorious."

It had happened just like that. All along Rei had a dark feeling that this would happen. Almost as if she had been waiting for it to happen without wanting to realize. One of them would die. Or both. She wondered what would happen to Storm without his brother and what he might be going through emotionally.

The entire crowd had died down and was silent. There were now 17 scarfs claimed. Now that Bolt was finished, everyone was beginning to lose interest. Some were walking away, preparing to head to the Arena of Kings for the second trial.

Rei felt a hand on her shoulder. "I'm sorry, Rei," said Lucius. She could feel the sadness in his voice. "I wanted to believe it was possible ... but who were we kidding? We are Curseborn after all." He lowered his voice at the word. "This is why we don't fight in the games Rei ... because we would just die out there." Dewey was silent at their sides. He looked to Rei but couldn't bring himself to say anything, not that he knew what he might say even if he did.

"Don't say sorry to me!" Rei snapped, a tear slid down her cheek. Lucius moved back slowly and stared at the fire in her eyes.

"I'm not the one who just lost a brother! Apologize to Storm and tell him you didn't believe in him or his brother from the start!" Tears flowed stronger than ever down her cheeks, "If you had just poured your energy into believing in their survival, into believing in them, then maybe ... just maybe ..." She fell to her knees. Her palms hit the cold ground.

"I don't want to believe it," Rei choked, trying desperately to hold back the tears. She couldn't even feel the tears anymore. She could feel nothing. It had only been one passing of Day and Night since Caim and Storm had saved them in Melri's. Caim was so powerful. He was so pure. And now he was gone. Forever.

She looked up at the sky, tears glistening like crystals into a puddle on the cold stone.

"Please ... don't let it end like this."

- - - -

Silence surrounded Caim. No, not silence. A strange eerie whooshing sound was all that he could hear. The energy all around him was real, like a misty fog. He was floating, but he could not discern any movement in any direction. His eyes fell on Mortal Aeryx beneath. Only a thick darkness returned his gaze.

LI – THE FINAL 18

Caim floated around while reaching his arms out in front of him, trying to grab onto something, anything. In the distance his eyes focused on several large shapes floating in the stillness. As he stared closer, his eyes widened. There were bodies of dead Sorians all around him. Dozens. No, hundreds. There were so many he couldn't tell. Thousands?

"Where am I?" he called, and no one answered. Above him he could see the clashing of energy, or rather, he could feel it. It felt like two enormously powerful energies fighting against one another. A sudden eerie voice spoke to him from the calm.

"Another one has come to live among us ..." whispered one of the bodies. Caim whipped around to see an old man floating amongst the bodies; long silver hair flowed past his ankles and his eyes had a cold, defeated look within them. He could feel barely any presence from the man.

"I will never live here," said Caim, clenching his fist. He looked all around.

"You have no choice," whispered the old man. "None can leave this place. You have but two options. Take your own life, or choose to believe that one day someone, anyone, will come for us. But you would have to be a foolish old man to believe such nonsense. None will ever come, for there is no way to ever leave this place."

"Doesn't matter if no one can leave," said Caim. "My brother needs me. And I won't die here."

Caim looked around and realized that dozens upon dozens of the bodies had dried blood upon their necks, or swords wrenched into their chests. They were lifeless and still. But beyond the dead were others who looked dead. They were silent and still and gazing at him. They were inviting him. Inviting him to a place where none could ever leave.

"Welcome to the end of your life, or the beginning of merely existing," the old man muttered. "With our immortality we cannot die despite lack of food or water. Our bodies wither but only we can make the choice to take our own lives. It is a terrible fate. It is a fate I would wish for no one, not even my worst enemy."

Caim took a long hard look at the scene around him.

After a minute, he took the deepest breath he could possibly manage, raised his arms to the sky and roared as loudly as he ever had.

"I'M GOING BACK TO SORIA!!!"

The old man smirked and closed his eyes, "they always start out like you. But with time you will come to see the hopelessness of where we are. Go on. Try. See for yourself what it is that you must defeat to leave this place."

Caim looked up and down at the torrential flashing of energy. It was truly a power beyond anything he had ever felt. "I wonder if the Dragon King has power like this ..." he whispered to himself. Without taking the time to think about his question, Caim surged his aura and raced towards the clashing energy. With a hard smack, Caim hit a wall that forced him backwards with three times the force until he was once again floating calmly.

"Dammit, that hurt!"

The old man sighed, "It is hopeless boy."

Caim screamed and swore as he tried harder and harder to fly back into Risia's field. But every time he came close the force outside the Calm Zone knocked him backwards with a power that he could not contend with. Wind currents rushed around his body like a tornado as he forced his entire being into breaking free. His eyes grew brighter and brighter as he screamed, unleashing all the caged aura of his body.

It wasn't working. He fell back, short of breath. The pains in his body were getting worse. The realization of his doom was coming upon him, yet he wouldn't take the time to even consider it. He couldn't consider it. If he did, all hope would truly be lost. He would break free. No matter what.

There was only one way left to him. He didn't want to have to use it here, but he had no choice. *I'm out of options, I have to use it. I just hope it's enough!*

Caim crouched down and threw his right arm out to his side. *"Aura Drive!"*

The clashing auras of both Magnetic Barriers began to ripple like water. The ripples grew steadily bigger until shards of brilliant blue energy started breaking off, hundreds of them. Soon there were thousands. They floated through the air and wound their way up Caim's arm. He could feel the energy fueling his body. More and more he focused his technique, breaking down the energy of the barriers and absorbing it into himself.

The old man raised an eyebrow. Others amongst the dead turned to look at Caim. In their eyes was only hopelessness. And even within their hearts, they feared glimpsing hope for the fear of it being taken away. But still, they looked.

From Caim's shoulder began to grow one long and sharp wing, cackling with the ardent energy of everything he was absorbing. The wing was the same brilliant blue as a silver blade before a crystal moon. Sharp and clear it rose from his right shoulder as he stood. Opening his eyes; they gleamed like silver fire.

Caim flexed his arms, feeling the enormous power rushing through him. His Limit Seal had never worked in such a way before. The energy of Mortal Aeryx was unlike any energy he had ever felt. It was not just powerful, but ancient, as if it were a type of energy that had grown in strength over long ages of sitting dormant. A godlike force. Exactly what he imagined the Dragon King's energy to feel like. He could feel it whirling through his body, fueling his every nerve, strengthening his every sense. But the greatest difference in its power was that it was unending. The two energies of Soria and Mortal Aeryx contained so much chaotic energy that no matter how much Caim siphoned from them, they would never deplete. And because of this, Caim's aura cage began expanding beyond what it had ever been.

With one last glance down, he felt the single wing rise powerfully from his shoulder, and he rose. All around him the bodies of the dead seem to awaken, their eyes rolling open and their mouths twisting into grins. Each of the dead bodies began to fade away into nothing but energy that fed into Caim's body, as if their once lost dreams of escaping would be achieved through Caim. The dead were relinquishing their last remaining spirit force to him.

"I'll be ..." whispered the old man.

"Lend me your energy," roared Caim. "And I will free you! I cannot do it without your belief!" Amongst those who had chosen not to take their lives, they felt a fire rising in their souls. A fire that was kindling something they thought had been lost forever. A glimmer of spark could be seen from their eyes as they rose around Caim.

"Rise, boy!" Voices began to chant around him. "And free our spirits forever! If you are our only hope then so be it! If you are a descendent of the Living Blades, a hero sent from above, so be it! Take what you need of our energy and free our spirits forever!!!"

"I WILL!!!!" Caim roared. His voice crackled into the energy of the first barrier, sending a shivered crack up through it. The old man stared in awe at the force of Caim's voice, and then smiled.

"You'll need more than that I'm afraid," he spoke.

After a long deep breath, Caim crouched down, pulled forth his blade and focused all his energy into its edge. A blazing fire enveloped the Fallblade and with all his newfound energy, Caim shot up and slammed into the barrier of Risia like a spear hurled by the God of War. The bubble bent as he struck it but he was not thrown back as he had before. Slowly, he began inching forward. The force made the fifty-fold weight feel like nothing. It was as if Risia had been transformed into a demonic being, and was holding him down with a hand the size of the moon. He could feel the energy shredding through his skin. Blood was seeping from his wounds and swirling all around him, but still he was rising. He felt as if the power of the world were grasping his ankles, pulling him down, condemning him.

But still he rose.

The dead became nothing but spirits who fed Caim's spirit.

The living released all they had to give and began to chant.

"Rise! Rise! Rise! Rise!"

"I won't give up!!! I won't ever give up!!!" Very slowly,

Caim began to climb through the twisting field of magnetic energy. His aura was radiant all around him, his eyes blazing bluer than ever before. The barrier cracked. Hard.

Suddenly he felt himself fall an inch. Then another. And another.

"No!!!" Caim cried. He felt a presence upon his shoulder. It was the presence of the old man.

"I've been waiting for someone like you," said the old man. "Waiting for someone I could give all of my last remaining energy too. Someone that can save all of our helpless souls! Take what I have been holding for all these cycles! TAKE IT AND FREE US!!!"

Caim felt one final surge of ancient energy come into his body. Pushing harder than ever, Caim didn't flinch as three ribs shattered in his body. His wrists, his arms, his legs, everything was on the verge of destruction. Forcing everything he had, his aura doubled and tripled in size, his wing becoming a solid expanse of blue flame. Caim felt his speed increasing as he shot further and further upwards—the Calm Zone pulled violently at him from beneath, begging him to stay and live forever in the realm of nothing—but with one final scream, Caim felt his body rip through the Magnetic Field and shoot back into the realm of Soria.

The old man closed his eyes smiling and fell, never to be seen again.

"You've come ... finally." were his last words.

- - - -

Storm's eyes flashed open.

- - - -

Lady Scylla, Lord Falkor, Sakura and Vasuki cast their glances in the same direction. An enormous power had just entered the fields of Risia.

"Impossible ..." said Lady Scylla.

The Empress turned quickly. "What happened?"

Lady Scylla's eyes were wide in disbelief. "It cannot be … but it is true. The boy who fell to the Calm Zone … has returned!" Sakura's eyes were wide in disbelief. "How can that be?" she muttered. She felt something else leave the Calm Zone behind the boy. Dozens of auras. *No, more.*

"He's freed them," whispered the Empress.

— — — —

Caim erupted out of the Calm Zone. The pressure of passing through the barrier launched him upwards as if he had been fired from the barrel of a gun. His eyes grew sharp, focusing on his target. In the far distance he found what he sought. Bolt was floating just beyond the bottom of Risia. Their eyes locked. Behind him hundreds of Sorians flew forth from the crack in the barrier where Caim had punched through. They rose behind him like an army of the dead.

Caim's *Aura Drive* rapidly absorbed energy from the hanging vines, the blue shards fueling his single flaming wing. Everything Caim drew near disintegrated from his raw auric pressure. He flashed upwards like a shooting star aimed for the sun. Bolt immediately turned and took off, flying with all his might towards the distant black bridge.

"LET'S DO THIS, BIRD!!!"

A moment later, Caim burst out from under Risia, rising fast after the nowl and closing the distance between them. He could see the silhouette of the massive bridge growing larger, and a strange pointed tip resembling an upside-down tower descending from directly beneath the Arena of Kings.

The announcer's voice roared across Soria. "IMPOSSIBLE! THE IMPOSSIBLE HAS HAPPENED! THE CONTESTANT HAS PASSED BACK INTO THE REALM OF SORIA AND IS GAINING ON BOLT. HE LOOKS LIKE AN ARROW OF PURE BLUE FIRE!! HOW COULD HE HAVE BROKEN FREE OF THE CALM ZONE!? WHO IS THIS SWORDSMAN BOY

WHO HAS STOLEN MY HEART!? AND ARE ALL THESE SORIANS EMERGING FROM THE CALM ZONE SURVIVORS WHO HAVE BEEN TRAPPED DOWN THERE FOR WHO KNOWS HOW LONG!? IT SEEMS A HERO HAS EMERGED!!!"

All of Soria froze in awe, watching, as all the airvras of the land switched to the image of Caim rushing after Bolt straight up to the bridge. Children held their parents' hands tightly as everyone held their breath. Cheers began rising from the distant edge of Falia all the way through Risia.

Caim could feel the heaviness of the wind weigh down upon his body as he shot upwards. He could see Bolt struggling to pick up speed but his wing motion seemed sloppy.

Caim sheathed his blade, "Weren't expecting me to come back, were you!?" He could feel the beating of Bolt's heart, which was rapidly increasing. The edges of Falia and Risia were passing by in an instant. Caim could see the bridge above him become larger and larger.

"Here we go!!!" the announcer shrieked. "The final stretch! If the contestant allows Bolt to pass the bridge, it's all over! He's coming up fast and passing the bottom half of Falling Tower! Any second now they will explode past the bridge! This is it! If he catches Bolt, he will be the 18th contestant to claim his scarf! It's now or never!!!"

"BOLT!!!" Caim screamed. Deep within his body something snapped, as if the cage of his aura had long since been dormant and had finally been awakened. Seconds remained. The wind screamed against his face.

"10!" *Soria began chanting …*

"9!" *Their breath grew light and their eyes widened…*

"8!" *Caim reached his hand forward …*

"7!" *Rei held her breath …*

"6!" *The Empress locked her hands together …*

"5!" *Storm closed his eyes …*

"4!" *Bolt squawked furiously …*

"3!" *The bridge came above them …*

"2!" *Caim stretched out his fingers …*

"1!" *A hurricane of wind exploded past the bridge …*

Caim and Bolt erupted past the edge of the bridge and Caim's energy caused every Sorian watching to stumble and fall backwards. Caim and Bolt vanished from everyone's eyes.

Everyone grew silent across Soria. Even the announcer was quiet. Storm leaned with his arms crossed against the side of the coliseum. He looked up for a moment, then looked back the ground and closed his eyes.

—   —   —   —

"Did he catch him!?" Rei shouted. Lucius was quiet. Dewey's mouth was hanging wide open. They stared intently into the airvras before they noticed a speck above the bridge falling down towards it. "What's that?" Rei whispered, gripping Lucius's hand tightly.

—   —   —   —

High above the bridge, a silhouette appeared, flipping backwards through the air, his legs perfectly straight. All watched in silence as the silhouette back-flipped out of the sky and landed softly on his feet. He crouched down, his back turned.

Everyone in Soria held their breath as Caim stood up. His hands were empty. He turned and grinned—clenched within his teeth was none other than the black scarf with the symbol of a lightning bolt in the center. In that moment, hundreds upon hundreds of Sorians who had escaped the Calm Zone with Caim flew up and landed on the side of the bridge. Their eyes were full of tears. Some fell to their knees. Their energy was cloaked with the feeling of the dead, and it sent chills through contestants who stood close to them. They were like ghosts who had risen once again.

All across Soria cheers erupted. Some were crying, others kissing and running through the streets. It was the loudest Soria had ever cheered. Elation rushed through the lands of Falia and Risia. The impossible had happened. A new champion had been born. Bolt had been caught.

- - - -

Even the Empress was awestruck. First one tear, and then others fell down her cheeks. "Wonderful," she whispered, "simply wonderful!" She turned and did a spin, nearly tripping. "That was incredible! We cannot believe it!

Absolutely amazing! Look how many of us he has saved by escaping that dreadful place!"

Lady Scylla turned her eyes to Lord Falkor. "I still cannot believe it. It should be impossible for anyone to pass through the Calm Zone. Hard to believe we haven't heard of this contestant before. Who is he?"

Lord Falkor was beaming. Sakura was dumbfounded, unable to move or to think. Vasuki merely grinned evilly, anxiously awaiting his meeting of the contestant that had stirred his fighting spirit.

- - - -

The announcer was trying to speak through his own surging elation. "My fellow Sorians, the nowl we all thought was impossible to catch, rivaled by none, the King of Nowls—has been caught! Bolt has finally met his match! And what a match that was! But beyond the catching of Bolt, it would seem that this boy has saved the lives of hundreds of Sorians who have fallen victim to the Calm Zone. Without him, they would surely have waited forever in that terrible place we can only imagine. Ladies and gents, please, give it up for our young contestant! You, young man, are an inspiration to us all!!"

Caim stood tall on the edge of the bridge smiling and laughing. Despite his elation, he felt like he was about to faint. The fatigue of his overuse of *Aura Drive* was catching up with him. But he would not faint. Nor even kneel. He had never felt like this in his entire life. The pain was nothing. Dozens of Sorians surrounded him, cheering for him as he raised the black scarf of Bolt high in the air. All of the nowls from the race descended out of the sky and landed on the edge of the bridge. Bolt caught Caim's eyes and he bowed his head, never taking his prideful eyes off his rival. All of those from the Calm Zone turned to him and bowed. After a moment, many of them took to the skies, returning to the world of the living.

"Well, well, well everyone!" started the announcer. "A hero and a legend!!! It seems we have launched off to a spectacular start to this cycle's Soldier Games! And my, what a start it was! I don't know whether to call it luck or skill but either way I am completely astounded, as I'm sure you are as well! This is by far, the greatest Chasing of the Scarves I have ever seen!!!" He wiped a tear from his eye. "I have always dreamed of announcing the games when Bolt would be caught, and now I have! It's a dream come true!! Thank you!!!!"

"YOSHA!!!!" Caim screamed as loudly as he could to the clouds above.

- - - -

Rei turned to Lucius, tears running down her face. Yet, the tears were different this time. She couldn't explain her happiness. For Storm, Caim, and for all of those who had been saved. She thought she had lost somebody she truly loved. She blinked, realizing how close she felt to Caim and Storm. She loved them both. For everything they were. For everything they stood for. And for everything they would change. She took a deep breath.

"Hope," she said. "Caim … Storm … they are the bringers of hope."

Lucius shook his head. "I don't know what to say …"

Dewey was still completely awestruck, "Wait … but how? That's impossible … I remember my dad telling me stories about the Calm Zone when I was a child. He said that not even the Living Blades could have escaped that place …"

Rei smiled from her heart, "you can ask him how he did it after they win the games." She turned to Lucius, "there is nothing to say. Not when you see something like that. Songs will be sung and poems will be written of this moment for all the ages to come of Soria. All I know is we are going to the Arena of Kings to watch the end of this!!!"

"I wonder if they're even Sorian," Lucius muttered.

"Seriously," answered Dewey. "That's unreal. He just made history!"

LI – THE FINAL 18

Rei looked up at Caim on the airvras grinning, "They're Curseborn, remember?"

Lucius couldn't help but grin. "I guess they are. We are."

"And now, without further ado," said the announcer, "we have identified the final 18 that will pass on to the second trial of the Soldier Games. The terrible, haunted and daunting Ascending of Falling Tower!!! Good luck brave contestants, and may the light of Vale shine upon you! The second challenge is about to begin!!!"

Glossary

firm age for the tryouts

Cloud Rider Aurelius – the referee of the Chasing of the Scarves trial

Dewey – childhood friend of Lucius and Rei

Einstein – an extremely intelligent nowl that has only ever been caught by Lady Sakura

Empress Aurora Ne'Fair – the Empress of Soria

Fang – Princess of the Flares

Flaps – one of the guards of the Bridge that Ties Worlds

Galfanon (Gal-fa-non) – A majestic creature known as a Chameleoth

Galileo – one of the Firstborn, and the original creator of Alchemy. Disappeared long ago in search of a cure for the mysterious curse

Gene – leader of the infamous Rogue X

Graelsi (Grale-cee) – old woman and owner of the Enchanted Stone Alchemy Shop

Grandmaster Arius – Strategic Elder to the Empress

Kaekol (Kai-cole) – the greatest dishwasher and pebbles player in all the lands

Kodi – (Ko-dee) a member of the infamous Rogue X

Kreitos (Kray-ee-tos) – A Kushala Flare, and Kin to the Master of the Forest

Ladon – a young inventor bent on fulfilling a promise to cure the disease Break

Lady Aquas (Ah-kwus) – Rank 6 of the Force

Lady Arya (Ar-ee-uh) – Rank 4 of the Force

Lady Enies (N-E-S) – Rank 9 of the Force

Lady Sakura (Saw-ku-ruh) – Vice Captain of the Force

Lady Scylla (Sill-a) – Captain of the Force

Lady Theresa (Teh-ree-sah) – Rank 5 of the Force

Lady Vale (Veil) – The Goddess of Life

Lady Zeila (Zay-luh) – Rank 8 of the Force

Lithael (Lih-thale) – Guard of Force Tower

Lord Falkor (Fall-core) – Captain of the Shield

Lord Felwin – Rank 3 of the Shield

Lord Galileo – a firstborn and renowned creator of Alchemy

Lord Vasuki (Vah-su-key) – Vice Captain of the Shield

Lucilin (Lu-sy-lin) – organizer of the Falian tryouts

Lucius (Lu-shus) – brother of Rei

Maile (My-lee) – Adopted daughter of the Empress; youngest of the three sisters

Master Atreyu – one of the seers of the airvras

Melri (Mell-ree) – owner of the restaurant, Melri's

Miss Shareiya – Dewey's mother, and owner of the shop Colossus Hunters

Mr. Waddles (Wah-duls) – A strange looking bird creature imprisoned by the Force Corps for reasons unknown

Noctis – a nowl and close friend of Kodi

Old Meaty – the vendor who sells meat to Kodi

Rakaella (Ruh-kay-la) – Guard of Force Tower

Rei – (Ray) – sister of Lucius

Remi (Reh-mee) – Adopted daughter of the Empress; oldest of the three sisters

Rinwarth – a noble, and Anima's second in command

Ronin (Row-nin) – Grandfather of Caim and Storm

Shin – one of the guards of the Bridge that Ties Worlds

Skypro – the greatest server in the sky

Sora (Sor-uh) – Unknown

Squall Risier – a deadly swordsman and wielder of the blade, Daybane

Storm – Brother of Caim and Grandson of Ronin

Virtuoso Jiselangelo – a firstborn and legendary artist known for his living mural within the castle

Wicked Witch – an evil witch who manages the restaurant, Melri's

Woolith – a noble, and Anima's third in command

<u>REALM OF SORIA</u>

Aquas Eternis – the great tree of Risia, and keeper of the world's memories

Arena of Kings – the coliseum in which they hold the Soldier Games. Sits on the center of the Bridge that Ties Worlds

Aurora's Light – The white castle of the Empress, and the Capital of Risia

Bakonia – a great creature of darkness that rises from Mortal Aeryx to eat the moons

Bridge that Ties Worlds – the bridge that connects the worlds of Risia and Falia

Calm Zone – a place between the magnetic barriers of Risia and Mortal Aeryx. A place of no return

Cataclysm's Touch (Ka-tah-klism) – A great cleft left in Falia by the God of Earth's axe

Death's Edge – home planet to the God of Lightning, Son Raiden

Enchanted Stone – an Alchemy shop owned by a very old woman named Graelsi

Falia (Fall-ee-uh) – The Eastern Wing of Soria

Force Tower – The tower of the Force Corps

Lasilia – the capital city of Risia

Mako Village – a small village of hunters on the outskirts of Neverend Forest

Neverend Forest (Neh-ver-end) – A magical forest gifted upon Falia by the Goddess of Life

Nocturnis Aqua (Nok-turn-iss) – The great tree of

Falia, and keeper of the fallen spirits

Relic Room – a room within the castle that contains many treasures of Soria

Risia (Riz-ee-uh) – The Western Wing of Soria

Senyria Lake (Sen-ee-ree-uh) – A magical lake gifted upon Falia by the Goddess of Life; holds healing properties

Soria (Sor-ee-uh) – The two lands floating in the sky where the Sorians live

Spearway to Eden – the main tower of the castle and home to the Empress

Starseeker, Tower of the Damned – a mysterious tower on the outskirts of Risia

Thousand End Caves – a myth that lies somewhere beneath the realm of Falia . . .

Trestles (Tressles) – the Capital of the floating world Falia

Vale's Garden – Home to the Goddess of Life

Valyti (Va-lee-tee) – The secret training grounds of the Force Corps

UNIQUE TERMINOLOGY

Aethir Ring (A-thur Ring) – The first solar system. Home of the Sorians and Seven Gods

Airvras – a bubble of aura that is used to project live action

Alchemy – a magical process of transformation, creation or combination

Alkahest – the universal solvent, and the ultimate tool of deconstruction

Ascending of Falling Tower – a trial of the Soldier Games

Aura – The energy within a Sorian; can be seen in the form of different colored energy flames

Black Games – a term used for a tournament where all contestants are killed

Black Rains – the flare's nickname for Storm

Blood Aura – Storm's Limit Seal

Break – a mysterious disease that puts those inflicted to sleep eternally

Chasing of the Scarves – a trial of the Soldier Games

Colossus Hunters – hunters who track and hunt terrifying and enormous creatures

Curseborn –a timeless curse that has no cure

Cycle – Equivalent to one century

Daybane – a blade with a mysterious connection to the dead

Dragon King – the greatest myth of their world. No one really knows who or what it could be

Elementa Rings – Alchemic rings that give the user elemental abilities

Eiendrahk (A-in-drawk) – The dark and never-ending war between Death and Life

Enhancers – Sorians used to create the smoke rings for the Chasing of the Scarves

Firstborn – the first and only sons and daughters of Night and Day

Fallblade – A greatsword of the past with two different forms

Great Laws of Soria – the four great laws of Soria including the Law of Sacrifice, Law of Blood, Law of Sky and Law of Challenge. They rest in the form of crystals within Vale's Garden

Hollow – A bone-type exoskeleton armor that grows on the skin of Sorian's bodies

Inner Depths – The world within one's mind that is made up of their past, and emotions

Jonken – a game played often to settle a dispute

Language of the Eldest – also known as the Language of the Gods. The original and first language of the Universe

Limit Seal – A unique, hidden ability that each Sorian is born with; only the strong-hearted can learn them

Living Blades – the original heroes of Soria. The seasons were created and named after each of them. They are Fall, Winter, Spring and Summer

Lunar Rising – A sword technique of Storm's

Nowl – a celestial creature and ancient ascendant to owls

Omni Stone – an Alchemic gem that temporarily grants the user invincibility

Philosopher's Stone – the stone of rebirth, and the ultimate tool of reconstruction

Projectors – Sorians used to control the airvras that display the games to those around Soria

Raising of the Flags – a trial of the Soldier Games

Ring – Equivalent to one year

Rogue X – a mysterious organization of Curseborn plotting against Risia

Rose's Echo – the most famous rock band on Soria

Sacred – the spirit of a creature whose energy has been crystallized into their heart, leaving behind a very unique and powerful gem

Shade – Equivalent to one hour

Silvers Fangless – the flare's nickname for Caim

Soldier Games – The Two Worlds Tournament of Soria; held once every 10 cycles

Sori – the currency of Soria

Starless Night – The final attack of Caim's Fallblade in its second form. A great wave of energy that is fired from the blade

Stone of Sky – an Alchemic gem that temporarily allows the user to fly

Sun and Moon Council – a council of those who oversee the two worlds

Tree Spirits – little creatures that are born of the Great Tree's spirit

Tri-Force Stone – an Alchemic gem that vastly improves strength, speed and stamina. Can only be used 3 times

Two Worlds Tournament – the olden name for the Soldier Games

Weavelocks of Fate – three mysterious mirrors woven of string that are used to glimpse the future

Winged Key – proof that one has passed the tryouts. Grants access into the Soldier Games as a contestant

A special preview of the next volume in the

FOUR LORD'S

High fantasy epic,

NOVELLA IV:
FALLLING TOWER

The riveting sequel to

THE TWO WORLDS TOURNAMENT

Available for purchase December 1st, 2015

LII - The Pact

Aurora's Light, the White Castle. The birthplace of legend— home to the Empress of Soria and quarters to the greatest warriors in all the land. It is guarded night and day by an elite team of soldiers. Infiltrating the castle is a suicide call, and thus its walls have never been breached.

Kodi stood silently on top of one of the four inner towers of Aurora's Light, quietly catching her breath. The tip of the tower was nearly thirty feet in diameter, with all black stone at her feet. In the center of the tower floated a strange black orb; her eyes rested momentarily there before glancing elsewhere. The outer rails were tall, taller than her (which wasn't saying much) and riveted at their edges. From where she stood she could clearly see the other three inner towers in the distance, and in the center, reaching higher than any of them, the glistening diamond tower stood: the Spearway to Eden. In the center of the flooring was a circular ring carved into the stone about a foot deep. She took a deep breath. For now, she was safe.

The first part of her mission had been successful. She had flown, unnoticed by anyone, on the back of Noctis and discreetly dropped onto the tower where she now stood. If she didn't know any better she would have guessed that it was Lady Scylla's tower. The thought gave her chills. It wasn't long before she heard the announcer declare the end of the first event, and she knew that soon all Sorians—both of Risia and Falia—would soon be ushered into the Arena of Kings to take their seats.

Unzipping her dark jacket, she pulled out the scroll that had been given to her on the bridge. Two days before she had met with the leader of the Rogue X's, and had officially accepted the mission that all deemed impossible: infiltrate Aurora's Light and find the Relic Room. She knew not what lay within the Relic Room, only that it was kept completely sealed and guarded, always. She read the scroll.

The thief of legend has been born. You, my friend, are a badass.

If you are reading this you have successfully infiltrated Aurora's Light: a task never completed in all the ages of our history. You have taken the first step in becoming the greatest thief to ever live. However, everything is about to become infinitely more difficult. Use this map to make your way through the castle and rely on the skills you have acquired during your training. I trust what you have learned from us will be of use. Use any means necessary to distract the guards, but avoid unnecessary conflict. You are to be as covert as possible. Once inside the Relic Room, find the sword that belonged to the swordsman Fenrir, one of the special weapons forged by the great Blacksmith Masamune. It will have a blue bandana wrapped around its white sheath.

I also believe that you will find what you have been personally seeking all this time hidden within the same room. Our undercover agent in the castle has revealed there is a significantly high chance of finding it in the Relic Room. Good luck and may the eyes of Vale shine upon you.

Kodi's heart soared—was it truly possible that she would find what she'd been seeking for so long, her grandfather's book? She hoped more than anything it was the truth.

Within the scroll was another piece of rolled-up parchment that revealed a map of the castle. Kodi walked cautiously to the edge of tower and peered out. She could see clearly the other three towers, all the exact height as the one she stood upon; one at three o clock, another at twelve and the last at nine. In the center of them was her target, rising high above the rest. She arched her head back trying to see the tip.

She traced her fingers over the map as she carefully went over her plan. "Ok . . . If I'm on the southern-most tower, then it looks as if the Relic Room should be . . ." Her eyes glanced up from the map. "It should be somewhere within the Empress's Tower. Although I already know this, don't I. Why am I talking to myself?" She smirked, wondering if she was nervous.

She stared back at the diamond tower; many crystal windows with grand etchings of maidens and warriors ran up its sides. The stone in which it was built was the rarest and most indestructible of ore—Aurelian. Even the force of the great Lord Falkor wouldn't have been able to scratch the stone.

Kodi hesitated. Why would the leader of the Rogue X's want Fenrir's sword? Although it held extraordinary energy and was crafted by the fabled blacksmith Masamune, a powerful sword was only promising in the hands of an equally powerful swordsman. Was their leader truly so strong? And even if he was, what could one man do with one Epic? The tragedy of Fenrir was more than enough reason to believe that taking the same path was nothing more than a death call.

But there was another part of this mission. The parchment said that she would find what she had been seeking. *I never knew he had an undercover agent in the castle.* She rolled up the scroll and slid it back into her pocket. Feeling something else in her pocket, she pulled out a smaller scroll, and her elation sunk. It was an alchemic painting of her grandfather, a picture inscribed by means of alchemy onto a sheet of parchment. He had pure white hair with wise eyes and a carefree expression; wrinkles covered his fatigued yet joyful face. Beside him sat a young woman with beautiful waving brown hair and violet eyes; her face was perfect in complexion and her cheeks were soft and round. She smiled widely as if looking into the reflection of a happy future.

"Grandpa . . . I've come," Kodi whispered. "I've come to find your book. The one that will change everything. I made it this far . . . don't look at me like that. I'm not going back." Her eyes flickered to the girl with eyes like her own. "I hope one day I can be as beautiful as you . . ." She ran her fingers over the young woman's face so gently she felt she was touching her skin. "One day I'll find you too . . . mom."

She rolled up the parchment and placed it back in the pocket with the map. She smirked to herself. It wasn't as if she didn't have the entire castle's blueprint completely memorized already.

She turned her gaze back to the Spearway of Eden. The Relic Room had to be within the Empress's tower. It was the safest of the five, surrounded by the entirety of the Force and Shield; it would be virtually impossible for any to reach.

A sly smile curled her lips. Except for me.

Wasting no more time, Kodi stripped off her leather jacket, revealing a black catsuit that covered her entire body, feet and all. She carefully tightened each of the straps across her chest, fastening the leather links together. It was a special rubber material her grandfather had stumbled upon when experimenting with Raelic skin. One that was impervious to cold and heat. Taking a deep breath, she reached into her pocket and pulled out the ruby sphere.

She felt more anxious holding the little sphere than looking at the tower and preparing to break into it. The sphere was pure power in her palm, swirling with a mysterious ancient force, completely foreign to her. It felt warm in her hand, and she stared intently at it. She could feel its presence.

"This is it. Let's hope this works."

She reached her thumb up to her mouth and bit down until traces of blood were running down her finger. Taking a deep, deep breath, she held the sphere up before her, and slid her bloody thumb across its smooth face…

- - - -

Kodi felt as if she had fallen a thousand feet. Opening her eyes hazily she looked around, wondering where she was. All around her gnarled trees stretched up to a distant sky she could not see. It was not Neverend, nor any forest she had ever seen. The trees shimmered in and out of different shades of greens, silvers and golds. The ground was soaked in a foot of lukewarm water, murky and unreflecting.

She tried to speak but nothing came out. Looking closer, she found that out of all the identical trees, one was different. A strange slithering vine wound up its trunk past where she could see. Up and up it went.

For no reason she could identify, she felt as if she was supposed to climb that vine. When she grabbed the vine a strange sensation, as if something alien had come over her, made her instantly let go. But this was the only way. She grabbed the vine again and this time, started climbing.

Kodi climbed for what felt like shades with no end ever coming within sight. There were no branches on any of the trees, so she couldn't stop and rest at all. Before she knew it she couldn't see the ground. Fear started to grow within her like a darkness, yet she pushed it away and thought only of her grandfather. On and on she climbed, until her arms were shaking and her fingers bloody, but still she climbed, feeling as if she were climbing to the heavens.

"I can't go any farther! I thought I was supposed to meet the keeper of the Sacred! Are you even here!?" she finally cried. Everything was the same and no end was in sight. What if she hadn't chosen the right path? The forest of branchless trees felt ephemeral, like a forest from another world, another realm.

But she knew at this point she wouldn't make it back down. It was either up or fall. She forced her arms to keep moving

LII – THE PACT

one at a time. Sweat soaked her body and her fingertips were torn to shreds from the rough vine; the dried blood cracked as she moved and a great fatigue soon overcame her. Her eyelids started to droop as a sleepiness consumed her, but still she climbed. She had no way to tell what time it was because the condition of the trees never changed. Nothing but an eerie silence enveloped her. She suddenly felt her hand slip, and awakened from her dreamlike state. She slapped herself in the face. Falling asleep would be the end of her.

Finally, after shades of climbing, her eyes found something different. A light. Faint, but it was there. Kodi kept going, longing only for the light. Just when she felt she could go no farther and her darkest doubts were coming to fruition, the light opened before her, revealing the top and she ascended to the tip of the tree.

The top was completely flat, as if it had been cut off, and about six feet in diameter, leaving her only a few feet on each side. The view was like nothing she could have imagined. All of the trees around her had vanished suddenly, and there she was, standing on top of the highest point she had ever been on. The wind was soothing on her face, but the more she regained her energy, the more fear began to grow in her mind again. She closed her eyes tightly and breathed deeply. The fear began to dissipate. She was not afraid of heights.

Glancing down, confusion swept over her. The vine that she had climbed had completely vanished. There was no way down. She felt her heart starting to race faster and faster.

"Hello!?" she cried into the sky.

A voice of great strength, unmistakably male, growled back in her consciousness like a rumbling avalanche. "Who is it that has dared to enter this realm? I am Galfanon . . . and this is my world you have come unto. Who are you to enter my Sacred? And where is the boy that I bestowed my gift upon?"

Kodi trembled. "I am Kodi, sir. An alchemist. And I was traded your Sacred by the boy."

"Traded!?" he roared.

"Yes, sir." She didn't know whether or not to lie. She decided that honesty was the right path. "Yes, he traded me your Sacred . . . for a slab of meat." She flinched. The voice did not answer for a long moment.

"What an interesting boy, to trade something as precious as the soul of another for something as fleeting as a snack. I wonder, if he is merely foolish, or . . ." Kodi waited, but he did not finish his sentence. "And why have you come before me, young alchemist?"

"I wish to make a pact, Sir Galfanon!"

"A pact?" he bellowed. "You are merely a child! I have great-great-grandchildren twice as old as you. Surely you cannot expect one such as I to bind myself with you? What makes you think I would accept such a request?"

"I . . . I cannot allow you to say no, sir." She hesitated, wondering if she should have chosen her words more carefully. Well, no matter. It was already done.

The voice grew to a whisper, yet dark and powerful. "A pact is not something one agrees to for any simple reason. It is a binding of my power and yours. An attachment of my soul to yours and yours to mine. I see you have braved many treacherous trials, young one, and your quest doesn't appear to be close to ending. But still a shadow of doubt lies within you. There is a sense of urgency in your voice. A lack of patience. What is it you seek?"

"I seek only the power to change the world of Soria!"

He did not answer for some time. "That is a strange answer, young one, for Soria can be changed in many ways both good and bad. Yet I do not believe you intend to change Soria for the worse." Kodi nodded. "Yet how can I be so sure to trust your words? You come in a guise, cloaking your true intentions. I know there is something deeper that you are hiding from me. Why do you not come forward as yourself? Why do you hide behind that visage?"

Kodi felt as if she had been struck. Hiding behind a visage? What could she be hiding from him? She had come before him with an open soul, knowing that he would be able to learn things about her once she entered his world. Had she not come forward just as what he asked? As herself?

"I know not of what you speak, Sir Galfanon. I wear no visage. I seek only the power to change the world of Soria— for the better. I have searched a long time for one of your kin, Sir Galfanon. I urge you to believe I have no hidden agenda, no plans of betrayal. I am what you see. Nothing more, nothing less. I'm sorry I am not of greater strength to ask a pact of you."

"Do not lie to me, young alchemist!"

Kodi's eyes grew wide in shock. "I am not lying!" she shouted.

"You think to trick me? A master of camouflage at his own game? I do not take kindly to being lied to, young one. And I needn't remind you that you are in my world. These are my rules. You do realize that if you die within my world, your mind will die forever back in the realm of Soria. You will not make it out of here alive if you continue to try and trick one who is much older and wiser than you. Do not test my patience. Choose your next answer carefully, for I will not tolerate an adolescent mockery of what I know to be true."

Kodi collapsed to her knees. She knew not of what Galfanon spoke. What was she keeping from him? She sought only to make a pact with the great Chameleoth, to borrow his power for her long journey ahead. She desperately tried to find an answer, any answer that would allow her to keep her life. This was no longer a matter of forging a pact. She had angered the spirit of the Sacred. The wind around her grew stronger as her mind raced back and forth.

Finally, she stood up and clenched her fists. "I'm sorry if I angered you, Sir Galfanon. It was not my intention." She bowed her head. "But I spoke the truth. I am only myself and I –"

"But yourself is not who you are!" roared the Chameleoth.

"What does that mean!?" A tear raced down Kodi's cheek and fell to her boot. She closed her eyes. What could she do? A sudden burning feeling caused her eyes to flash open. The open sky was gone. Roaring flames engulfed her from every angle; the heat was unbearable, the licking flames slapping the trunk of the tree, rising towards her. All she could hear over the roaring fire were blood-curdling screams. Why was she trapped in an inferno? And why was it so familiar? Fear struck her like a sword to the heart. Kodi clutched her head and screamed.

Galfanon's voice was like death in her ears. "Why is it you fall before the flames? Do you know now that I know? I know all about you, Kodi. I have seen your past. And what a dark past it is!"

The inside of a dark wooden cabin came unto Kodi's mind; there standing before the front door was her grandfather, holding a small, leather-bound book. With a subtle wave and a faint smile, he opened it and walked away. Tears streamed down Kodi's face as she screamed for him not to go. Her voice could not be heard over the roaring flames.

"Will you still lie to me knowing that your secrets cannot be kept? They are no longer your secrets. Honesty is your only escape. Speak! Before the flames of that deathly fire consume you!"

Kodi was trembling, sweating heavily. The heat was singeing her hair, smarting her senses, awakening a long-lost fear that she had never understood. Why were the flames so familiar? Tears poured down her cheeks. Blood ran down her wrists from the puncture wounds of her nails sinking into her palms. Her entire body was shaking and her eyes glanced to the side of the tree. All she wanted was to end her pain.

"I . . . I don't know," she whispered. "But please . . . stop this. Please!" She screamed as loudly as she could. "PLEASE STOP THIS, GALFANON!"

The flames vanished abruptly. She stood alone upon the tip of the tree, trembling; blood soaked her wrists and tears streamed down her cheeks. Night had taken over the sky. Before her rose the great and beautiful Nocturnis Aqua, sparkling with celestial fires from its trunk and distant branches. An ocean of radiating stars littered the darkness

LII – THE PACT

above it. At the base of the thousand-foot-wide tree was a shimmering black lake, reflecting the many stars above. Thousands of tree spirits watched from the enormous curled roots of the tree. And in the center of the lake was a tiny wooden boat with a young girl and an old man.

"Mom . . ." Kodi whispered. The girl turned as if looking at Kodi. She had the same beautiful brown hair, the same piercing violet eyes. The old man was her grandfather, yelling at her mother. She watched her mother grab the edge of the wooden boat that could barely hold the two of them.

"What . . . is this?" whispered Kodi. Was this a memory locked away in her mind from long ago? Had she watched this from the shore of the lake as a child? Or was this a trick from Galfanon?

Her grandpa cried out again, and her mother dove into the black water, vanishing beneath the ripples. Seconds later the boat dissipated slowly into ash—along with the Nocturnis Aqua, the stars in the black sky, and the shimmering water of the lake.

Kodi kneeled alone on the tip of the tree, before an empty sky. She did not know what to think. What to do. She merely sat there, staring at her bloodstained hands. The flames . . . she could still only see those horrible flames.

"I don't . . . understand," she whispered.

The deep voice of Galfanon spoke, this time calm and reassuring. "Young alchemist . . . it would seem that I have had a change of heart. Sometimes the minds of the old don't meld well with the minds of the young. I have shown you grievous images in an attempt to disrupt your lies. But I see now that you have not been lying—not intentionally. There is a part of yourself that you can no longer find. And I believe that on your journey to change the world of Soria, you may find just what you have been seeking."

Kodi's eyes widened in disbelief. "So . . . you'll join me?"

Kodi saw something shimmer in the sky like glass reflecting the light of the sun. It vanished. But moments later in a different area she saw the shimmer, this time reflecting a deep gold. Peering closer, she thought she saw two bright eyes for a split second before they vanished. The shimmer grew closer, flickering like a thousand shards of broken glass. It passed into a cloud of silver, disappearing for a few seconds from all sight.

And then she saw him. No longer cloaked, no longer hiding. The ancient form of Galfanon emerged; both majestic and wise was the Chameleoth as he swam through the sky. Enormous gold wings lifted from his serpentine body; great azure feathers flowed from the top of his head as he focused his gleaming orange eyes upon her. His eyes were keen and strong yet kind and full of awareness; Kodi kept her eyes locked on his as he flew closer. She stood up as Galfanon flew in circles around her, slowly coming closer until he was wrapping his body around the tree. His powerful claws dug into the trunk; his gold wings folded down against his back as his snout came within reach of her arm. She could not take her eyes away from his.

"I have decided to embrace your request, Kodi. I once had a different form when I was alive, but only through meeting you has a new form come upon me. My scales have changed to gold, my wings are more powerful than they have ever been. Only when a Sacred meets its true pact master is one granted a form to take within his world. I have been alone until now, with only my thoughts, and have grown bitter at my lack of ability to return to Soria. I will help you with your dreams. And I will help you to find yourself."

"Find . . . myself?" asked Kodi, quietly stepping forward.

"Yes," answered Galfanon, his eyes unwavering. "There is much you still have to learn about yourself, Kodi. But I will be here to help you along the way. We will travel together as one. We will fight together as one. We will die together as one. And together, we will unearth your deepest secrets and change the world of Soria. I wonder if the revelation of your own truth will alter your dreams for the world. Only then will I truly know if I have made the right choice in choosing you . . . as my other half, and the master of my pact."

"There are so many things you are saying I don't understand," said Kodi, stepping forward once again. She could feel the hot breath of the Chameleoth before her, warm and soothing on her skin. His head was bigger than her entire body.

"In time, young alchemist, in time. Now, reach forward and touch me. Only then can we become one. The pact must be unanimous. This tree is your life, Kodi. The only aspect of my world that is not a reflection of myself. I have accepted it—I have accepted you. Now you must do the same. Do not be afraid. Come."

Hesitantly, Kodi reached her trembling hand forward and placed it on Galfanon; his scales felt of metal before a fire, but they did not burn. Gazing past him she watched as the entire world changed before her eyes. The sky closed in from above as if it were folding down into a tiny piece of paper. Shadows grew quickly on the horizons, engulfing all until she could only see Galfanon's gleaming orange eyes. She focused on them without fear as all faded to black.

\- \- \- \-

Kodi opened her eyes, breathing heavily. She was standing back on the top of the tower. Sitting before her was the ruby sphere, glowing and steaming. Slowly but surely, she inched her way towards it. Upon touching it, she felt her hand grow hot as coal and she could not let it go. A long gash opened on her forearm and the blood from her wound wove around her arm until it was circling around the sphere. She watched as the cut suddenly closed and steamed, creating a spherical scar. The ruby sphere had disappeared.

"We now share a Pact," spoke a voice in her mind. "I, Galfanon, have knit my Sacred into your heart. As I am now a part of you, my thoughts are a part of you, and the more powerful our bond grows, the more powerful you will grow. Utilize my powers well, and learn to understand their weaknesses. I now understand you more so than ever, and am glad to have given my Sacred to such a brave soul."

"Thank you," said Kodi, a tear rolling down her face. She stood to her feet. Something strange had overcome her body. Her senses were sharper than ever before. She could see much farther, and her hearing had improved as well. She found herself smiling widely, unable to control her excitement. She had the power of one of the Chameleoth living within her. She looked to the ground and felt the picture in her pocket. She would never be alone again. She wanted to cry out in happiness but she held back. She cast her gaze toward the Spearway to Eden, the tower of the Empress.

"It's time." Drawing on the new power from her body, she felt something change within. She gazed at her arms, which were now transparent and changing in color to match her surroundings.

"Cloak of the Chameleoth," she whispered, and a great grin curved across her face. She grasped her blue scarf, which was lying on the ground where Noctis had left, and wrapped it around her neck tightly. Even the scarf changed in color. She reached to her back pouch and pulled out a tiny black box bound by sleeted silver and gold runes.

A horrid scent consumed her heightened sense of smell. She nearly vomited. She struggled to pull out the slimy black tar that tried to wrap itself around her fingers as if it were alive.

Kushala snot was a rare substance and if concealed, would stay tar-like and sticky for long periods of time. However, shortly after touching air, it would stick to any surface and harden, becoming nearly unbreakable. She rolled the slimy stuff into two balls and stuck one to the top of the tower before her. With the second ball, she aimed for the Empress's tower and threw with all her might. Three hundred meters it soared like a dart. Her strength had increased as well. The sticky black ball stuck perfectly to the side of the wall right above the window.

Kodi pulled out a long thin throwing knife the length of her hand. Attached to the blade was a long piece of line that connected to a second blade. Taking aim, she threw the knife perfectly, watching it pierce the air before piercing into the black ball of hardening snot stuck to the tower.

"Breaking into Aurora's Light, are we?" The voice of Galfanon sounded intrigued. "We may just be dying together sooner than I thought."

"Don't say that," said Kodi, pulling up her scarf. "This is nothing for a thief like myself!"

She jammed the second knife into the black ball of snot, connecting the points. Taking a deep breath, she jumped up onto the edge of the tower. Dark black chains that seemed to grow out of the tower reached forward, passing her line of sight and connecting high upon the Empress's tower. Far below, she could barely see lines of white and green—courtyards and rows of trees.

"I can feel your trepidation, Kodi," warned Galfanon. "Focus."

"Bah! Is this what I'm going to have to deal with now?" Kodi grinned. "I can't focus with you telling me what to do every five seconds!"

She checked to see if the knife was stuck. It wasn't budging. She jumped up and found her balance on the line connecting the knives. The wind was calm but not dead. She tried not to look down as she ran along the thin line until she reached the end. She looked like a faint black star dashing through the sky. Just before reaching the other side, she dropped quickly, hanging on to the line by a couple fingers, and slid through an open window before rolling to her feet. She immediately took cover next to a wall. She hadn't made a sound, and her skin quickly adapted to its surroundings, concealing her from all but the keenest eye.

"First ever infiltration of Aurora's Light," she whispered. "Successful!"

A Little Piece
of Us

We are the Four Lords. Two brothers and two best mates who have learned that our minds will always and forever work at their best when you work with others. We are story tellers in trade, and we long to create something that has never been before. Something that will touch people's hearts and leave them breathless. We are just like you. We work normal jobs every day, and try desperately to find our way in this labyrinth we have all come to know as life. But for us, even in the toughest of times, and we all have them, it was always stories that kept us going. It is our passion. It is how we can live life, yet still create. We believe that stories are the heart of everything.

That's exactly why four years ago, we came together from the corners of this world and began working on our own story. "One of the greatest stories ever told." This is what we told ourselves we would create. We devote our lives to this. To give something back to the world after the artists of the past have already given so much. We would not be who we are without them. And in turn, are willing to stake our futures on creating something for others. We are artists. We may be irrational, reckless, and stupid at times . . . but we know how to love.

ABOUT THE AUTHOR

Taken in a Holiday Inn parking lot after Anime Expo 2015: Gabe (top left), Franco (bottom left), Shanks (middle), Cloud (right), and Sephiroth (top right)

Hey all! I can't believe it's already been three months since the last installment in the Curseborn Saga story. For me it's been a long ride these last few months. Here's a little bit of what's been going with me. I recently just moved out and am living in a house with 4 of my best friends along with my beautiful girlfriend Kristen. By the way one of those friends is Squall D. Ace of the Four Lords! Needless to say it's been awesome. Honestly, it's been a long time coming, since after I moved back to the states from Japan, I was living at home with my mother who was sick. I stayed to take care of her, but I also stayed because I really didn't know what I wanted to do with life. I started going back to school as a Japanese major, but it was soon after that I realized that what I knew more than anything, and what I loved more than anything, was stories. Once I made the decision to be a writer, I knew that school was no longer the path for me . . . and dropped out.

Yeah, I dropped out. I decided to choose my own teachers and learn from their literature: Eiichiro Oda and Tolkien to name a couple. I lived at home during the next 5 years where I created TCS with my brother Shanks, and my two best mates. I needed time to learn and a stress free environment. So I worked at a restaurant and wrote in coffee shops. But now that my mom has finally recovered and is back on her feet, along with the publication of the first two books, I decided that it was my time to be on my own again. And so I took the decision and left home. I'm still living in sunny San Diego not far from my family, but it is such a good feeling to be on your own. I had nearly forgotten what it felt like.

On another note, I've still been rock climbing adamantly, along with training Muay Thai again (I trained for about 2 years when I was just out of high school with Heath "Cowboy" Harris). I've also recently bought a Suzuki GSXR 600, which is a motorcycle that is way faster than anyone really needs. I grew up racing and building cars so I feel comfortable at high speeds, and I feel as if I've developed a natural sense of caution for the rode and other drivers. Just to mention something, if you ever meet someone who rides, they probably don't want to hear that they are going to die. Just saying. Start off with the positives alright? Other than that, we as Four Lords were recently invited to Summit Series, which is a meeting of entrepreneurs in the middle of the Atlantic Ocean sometime in November. We are more than excited to be a part of such an adventure and feel very grateful for the opportunity! Anyways, that's what is new with me these days. I hope you enjoy the third novella in the series, it's a fun one for sure. I gotta run to pick up Kristen from work. I'm taking her climbing for her first time today . . . I had to bribe her into going by saying I would go to trivia night with her later on. Haha, yeah . . . it's a trade off right?

Take care!!!

May the light of Vale shine upon you all!

~ Cloud

57520108R00140

Made in the USA
Charleston, SC
18 June 2016